...AND WHITE OWL'S FEATHER!

K M Murray

This is a work of fiction. Names, characters businesses, places, events, locales, and incidents are either the products of the author's imagination or used in a fictitious manner. Any resemblance to actual persons, living or dead, or actual events is purely coincidental.

Up the airy mountain

Down the rushy glen

We daren't go a-hunting

For fear of little men;

Wee folk, good folk,

Trouping altogether;

Green jacket, red cap,

And white owl's feather!

The Fairies 1850

William Allinghan 1824 – 1889

CHAPTER 1

For years she had convinced herself that what happened that night was merely a figment of an over active imagination.

What age were they? Seventeen, almost eighteen? Typical teenagers of the early 1950s living in a little Scottish coastal town, less worldly wise when compared with young women of the same age today. Louisa and Julie had been friends since they were toddlers, playing together, living their lives in a world of magical tales, sharing their toys and laughter.

They were inseparable until they were nine, then Louisa's parents were allocated a prefab on one of the new housing estates being built on farm and moorland high above the town after the war.

Julie's family, preferring to remain closer to sea level, chose to remain where they were.

The girls were upset by the thought of being parted, but their separation only lasted for two years, until they were old enough to attend the same high school where their close friendship resumed.

One Saturday during a typical northern November evening, miserably dark, cold and pouring from the heavens, just like all the other Novembers they had known, the girls and Julie's wee collie dog, Bob, sat huddled together in a shelter at the sea front along the Ashton Promenade trying to keep dry.

They weren't successful thanks to Bob who kept dashing up to the iron railings waiting for a wave to break. Every time a huge torrent of water came cascading over and he was soaked he would race back to the shelter, give himself a vigorous shake, then jump onto the seat to cuddle between both girls who shrieked and screamed.

Their usual routine on a Saturday afternoon was to dress in their best clothes, catch the bus to Greenock and wander along Hamilton Street inspecting the goods being offered for sale in the shop windows. A recently opened fashion store named Paige was the favourite, selling blouses and skirts, so removed in style and beauty from the austere looking offerings of war time and early post war Scotland was the favourite. Everything was well beyond what they could afford nevertheless both would stand admiring and planning what they would buy when they were rich.

A visit to Woolworths with its multiple counters of confectionary, washing powder and goods of every kind, was part of the ritual and never missed.

Woolworths was always busy, particularly on a Saturday when the inhabitants of nearby towns pushed through its doors looking for a bargain.

That particular Saturday, Louisa who had managed to shoulder her way through the milling shoppers to get to the counters that sold what she was looking for, stopped beside one of the counters close to the back of the store. She was in the process of sniffing a bar of lavender-perfumed soap when someone jostled her appearing to tug at her handbag.

"Ow!" she said as she pulled it closer.

"A gift", a throaty sounding voice whispered in her ear. Bewildered, she looked around and for a moment caught sight of a short figure dressed in a bright green suit, yellow waistcoat, wearing a red cap with a white feather moving furtively away from her to disappear amongst the crowd.

"Did you see that man?" she asked indignantly when she saw Julie.

"What's the problem?" asked Julie who had been busy buying a jar of 'Ponds Vanishing Cream'.

"A man pushed me I think he was trying to steal my bag", she patted it holding it close to her chest.

"Oh, you've got to be careful, it's so busy in here, you get pushed all the time. Well, he didn't get your bag so not to worry. Now, if you have everything you want let's have a milkshake at the BB Café".

Louisa, glad to get out of the suffocating throng made sure she had all the goods she had purchased and together they made their way the café where they could show one another their particular treasures.

An hour later when they emerged, a curtain of rain greeted them.

"Quick, there's the bus at the stop, if we get a move on, we'll catch it", and they both began to run, reaching it just before it moved off.

After tea and she helped wash and dry the dishes, Louisa

pulled on her raincoat and fastened her rain mate securely.

"Cheerio, I won't be late!" she shouted as she opened the door.

"No later than nine thirty", her father reminded her.

Pulling the door closed behind her, she opened her umbrella which was immediately blown inside out by a great gust of wind. After a number of unsuccessful attempts to get it the right way around she admitted defeat and pushed it behind the step before running to the bus stop.

When the bus arrived at the pierhead she saw Julie and Bob waiting in a shop doorway.

As there wasn't a dance at the Gamble Institute that evening, they'd had the choice between visiting the local one screen cinema, or sitting in one of the cafes along Kempock Street nursing a mug of Bovril or a glass of hot orange. However, even that slim choice was no longer available when they discovered they had already seen the film, 'Knights of the Round Table', at the Regal cinema in Greenock the week before.

"Looks like it's another visit to the café", Louisa sighed, pulling a face.

While they sheltered in the doorway, making up their minds about which café to visit, the rain stopped.

"How about a walk along Albert Road as far as the Prom before we settle down for the rest of the evening?" Louisa suggested.

"Sounds OK to me", agreed Julie and linking arms they set out in the damp sodium lit night.

All went well enough at first but no sooner had they reached the sea front at Ashton Promenade when the wind got up and the skies opened, the rain slanting down in stinging icy needles. Bob gave a loud bark

"Seemed like a good idea at the time", Louisa groaned.

"Quick! Run for the first shelter!" screeched Julie.

No sooner were the words spoken than Bob took to his heels racing them along the road.

There were a number of shelters along the Promenade, offering views in four directions. The wooden walls stretched half way behind slatted seats and glass window panes completed the rest of the wall from there to the roof. They were very drafty yet they did provide a little shelter from the rain that whipped up the Clyde.

The girls sat scrunched up beside Bob in the first shelter on the dimly lit promenade watching the waves as the now howling wind whipped them into a frenzy.

"Bound to be blue kelpies creating this storm. Waiting for stricken boats to sink and drown the sailors". Julie gave a shiver.

"Oh, but look at those white horses", Louisa marvelled as the white crested galloping waves were carried up river by the incoming tide. "I love watching them", she murmured, "if you look hard enough, you can see knights with their swords on high charging towards the enemy army".

Julie laughed, "Yes, and I suppose you are the maiden in distress waiting to be rescued".

"No you are. I'm one of the knights", Louisa answered disdainfully.

"You can't be a knight", Julie protested, "they didn't have women knights in the olden days".

"Of course there were women knights", for a moment Louisa wondered why she was so sure about this until her attention was caught up once more in the maelstrom being played out in her imagination.

She was leaning forward urging her mount onwards as she perched astride one of the chargers, sword aloft, blood up, hurtling towards the enemy, listening to the sounds of battle carried by the wind.

Suddenly Julie gave a loud shriek. Louisa jumped, brought back to reality with a vengeance.

"What's the matter?" she cried.

"I've just had a brilliant idea!" said Julie. "Do you fancy a trip in the ferry to Kilcreggan?"

Shocked, Louisa stared at her.

"What! You've got to be joking. In this weather?"

"What's wrong with the weather? You said you loved watching the white horses".

"Well, I do but it's pouring, the wind would knock you off your feet. Not only that, it's pitch black in the middle of winter".

"So we are going to sit here for the rest of the night? Oh well, I suppose we could always go back to the Lido".

Louisa groaned, "I can't face another hot orange at the moment".

"Well my bum's getting sore on this seat, I'm going to have to move", Julie complained.

Louisa felt guilty asked, "Do you think the ferry will still be sailing? It looks a bit rough out there".

Julie looked up hopefully, "It won't kill us to have a look, will it? It would be a change, do us good".

Louisa wasn't so sure, she loved the sea as long as she was not in it or on it, but not wishing to appear awkward she agreed.

"OK, let's have a look then", she said hoping the sailings had been cancelled.

Julie perked up considerably at that.

The moment they stepped outside of the shelter, a wave, as if it was just waiting for the opportunity, gathered up an armful of shingle and threw it over them.

Shrieking and laughing, they raced across the putting green towards the pavement where arm in arm, leaning into the wind they headed towards the ferry slip at the pier. Bob aware of an adventure was afoot bounced excitedly back and forth leading the way.

"Julie, you'll need to put Bob back in the house, he'll get sea sick", Louisa gasped, the wind snatching her breath. She was sure Bob understood what she had said because as soon as they got level with the gate of Julie's house he took to his heels racing past it. Fortunately, they saw Julie's oldest brother, leaning back into the wind making his way along the pavement towards them.

"Catch him Phil! Don't let him go!" they screeched like a pair of banshees.

"Why? Where are you going?" he asked suspiciously, grabbing a hold of Bob's collar.

"Just to the Ashton. He's too wet, he'd be better in front of the fire."

"Aye, all right, I'll take him. I might see you two there later. Behave yourself and don't do anything stupid".

"What? Us?" Julie's face was a picture of innocence.

"Thanks, you're a pal", they thanked him profusely as he and a reluctant Bob continued their journey home.

"That gives us about two hours to get to Kilcreggan and back," Julie inspected her watch. "I forgot, his leave's over, he's joining his ship tomorrow, going to Singapore".

An odd kind of bittersweet moment brushed across Louisa when she thought about Phil. He had been a big brother to her too, lifting her up when she fell, kissing the sore bits better, applauding both her and Julie's efforts at entertaining, treating them to the matinees and summer shows. He had been home for three months and she had become so used to him being there. She would miss him.

The rain had eased off by the time they reached the station entrance at the Pier Head. In the dull yellow gas light, they examined their purses.

"How on earth did this get there?" Louisa carefully pulled a white object from her handbag.

"What is it?" Julie peered over her shoulder, "Why it's a feather! It's beautiful. Look. A white owl's feather".

They gazed at the large white feather in Louisa's hand. "Where did that come from - apart from the owl", Julie asked. Mystified, Louisa shrugged her shoulders before returning it to her bag.

Carefully counting out their change they found between the two of them they had just enough to pay for return fares on the ferry, tuppence each for pier duties as well as two cups of tea and a bun from the café that lay just across the road from Kilcreggan Pier.

Julie looked at her watch, "Better make up our minds now if we are going, the ferry will be leaving any minute now".

Having decided it was fait accompli, Louisa grabbed Julie by the arm and amid shrieks of excitement, they raced across the pier towards the little boat.

"Wait for us! Wait for us!" they screeched as the sky opened once more.

The ferry was still docked at the landing stage. The tide was high and the boat was raised enough to provide a view of the skipper's head as he stood at the helm.

"Wait for us!" Julie shouted once more, her voice almost lost in the wind.

One of the deck hands shouted, "OK! We're waiting!" as he steadied the bobbing plunging vessel by holding on to one of the piles underneath the pier. He held out a hand to help the girls to climb over the gunnels onto the passenger seats along the side. Once there they stepped down into the hull and cuddled under a large tarpaulin cover.

The ferry wasn't very big, not that much more than twenty foot from bow to stern and Louisa wasn't too happy when she saw water lapping from the bilges through the bottom boards.

"Is that a leak?" she asked suspiciously pointing to the water.

"What? A leak? Of course not, have you not noticed it's raining", the hand's voice was almost drowned out by the racket coming from the tarpaulin roof part of which had been ripped off and was flapping uproariously in the angry wind.

As he spoke a torrent of rainwater descended, the deluge missing them by a few feet.

'Confirmed landlubber' must have been obvious from the distraught look on Louisa's face.

The hand took pity on her, "Here hen", he said, "take this. If you get worried about the boat sinking you can use it to bail out".

He picked up a small saucepan from the bottom of the boat and handed it to her.

"If you scoop up more than half a saucepanful at the one time, look," and he drew a finger along the inside of the pan to give Louisa an idea of the half way mark, "let me know. Alright?" He gave her a pat on the head, "Don't worry".

She felt a bit better but didn't know why.

Once they set sail the boat began to pitch and toss on the turbulent angry waves. Never before had the amount of water scooped up from the bottom of a boat been more carefully scrutinised.

It had seemed a good idea at the time, but trying to keep one's balance in stormy seas, the saucepan in Louisa's flailing hands acted like an uncontrollable weapon of destruction. She clouted Julie on the shoulder, herself on the cheek twice , and almost brained the deck hand before it flew into the air landing somewhere near the bow.

The storm grew in ferocity threatening to swamp the little boat.

Crawling forward she succeeded in grasping the pan when all at once, as if someone had thrown a switch, the turbulent seas suddenly grew calm, everything became deathly silent and even the air stilled.

Pulling herself upwards, her nose just level with the gunnels she was amazed by how still the water had become. Then, without warning, some yards away, the water began to move as open-mouthed she watched a shape beginning to emerge. It broke the surface gently at first, then with a great heave as something enormous below the surface displaced gallons of water. Transfixed she watched as the heads and necks of two enormous horses broke the surface reaching thirty metres high above the little boat.

"Kelpies!" she gasped unable to take her eyes from the vision.

As she gazed in amazement at the magnificent creatures totally devoid of metal headgear, she became aware of a number of blue figures holding to the mane of each horse.

"Storm kelpies?" she gasped, her heart racing with fear as the waves began to build once more. She remembered the stories about their power to create storms and how they were said to search for stricken boats to sink drowning those onboard.

The voice of one of the blue men reached across the now boiling sea to the skipper who stood proudly erect at the prow of the boat.

As she listened carefully she heard the figure speaking what appeared to be lines from a poem then challenging him to complete the verse.

Louisa caught her breath, "Please dear Lord", she prayed, "don't let the storm kelpies get us. Let the captain complete the verse or we will all be drowned".

During the short pregnant pause that followed, Louisa felt as if her life was held in the balance before the silence was broken by the powerful voice of the captain who carefully in a soporific tone, spoke a few more lines until he reached the end of the verse.

As if caught in an eternity Louisa watched and waited in the silence.
One of the blue man acknowledged the captain with a salute. Then the sea calmed and the heads of the horses with their blue riders slowly began to sink beneath the waves.

Louisa looked around for Julie was nowhere to be seen and hysterically she called her name. To her relief Julie's head appeared from under the tarpaulin, "Nearly there only about another ten minutes", she consoled. "Oh Julie", she cried, "I've never been so afraid in my life. Being so close to the Kelpies was bad enough but when the blue men appeared, I was sure we were going to be drowned".

Totally unaware of the drama that had been played out a few moments before, Julie frowned,

"What horses? What blue men?"

Concerned that the wallop her friend had given herself with the wayward saucepan was harder than she had realised she urged, "Take it easy Louisa", "You'll be all right. We're nearly there".

Hardly able to believe that her friend was unaware of what had happened Louisa looked towards the captain for confirmation. However, he merely placed a finger to his lips then smiled.

During the next fifteen minutes of the journey Louisa sat in a daze, upright on the seat, her arms resting along the gunnels in an effort to control them shaking as a misty curtain of rain fell from the sky.

When they reached their destination at last and she stood up Louisa found her legs would not support her.

She was aware of her feet but it was the bits between those and the rest of her body that were the problem, somehow those bits had been transformed into quivering jelly.

One of the deck hands seeing her plight helped get her upright and on to the pier.

Pulling Louisa's arm around her shoulder Julie supported her while she took odd prancing steps towards the pier master.

"Looks like you had a bad crossing hen?" he said sympathetically.

"Tell me", Julie replied while Louisa open-mouthed could only gape at him.

By the time they paid him their dues of tuppence each, Louisa's wobbly legs had begun to remember what they were there for and to make an effort to behave normally.

The moment they left the pier, as if by magic the rain stopped and a pale-yellow moon looked out from behind the clouds casting an eerie glow over the little row of cottages and the café standing across the road.

A large black cat sat watching them and as they approached gave a loud 'Meow' leaving Louisa with the distinct impression that he had been waiting for them.

CHAPTER 2

"Well, here we are. What will we do now?" Julie asked.
Then answering her own question, "How about the
café?" she pointed toward the word 'CAFE' painted in
large green letters at different angle above a wide
window, "I wonder if it's busy".
"We could have a look", Louisa agreed.
She looked around for the cat but it was nowhere to be
seen. Must have wandered off she decided.

Approaching the café their ears were assailed by raucous
laughter, singing and cheering that increased in volume
when the door opened suddenly and two elderly
gentlemen in green jackets, vainly attempting to hold one
another upright, spilled out on the pavement.
A walking stick, a red cap and what looked like a large
pipe flew out after them.
"An' don't come back until yous learn to behave!" a
rough female voice roared before the door banged shut
once more and the pale glow cast on the pavement by the
bright yellow light inside disappeared.

"That's my kind of woman". The shorter of the two men cried admiringly as he blew a kiss towards the door. "Stand still can't you", the taller one gasped as he attempted to steady himself by placing one hand on top of his companion's head, while at the same time stretching the other downwards towards their belongings. "It's not me, it's you", the shorter man wheezed through helpless, inebriated laughter, "Either that or I've got a wobbly head". He fell on to his knees 'he-hawing' like a demented donkey.

The taller man successfully grasping the pipe stuck it into his own mouth and began to make noisy sucking sounds as he struggled to drag his companion back to his feet.

At last, successfully pulling him upright, he pushed the cap onto his friend's head so that it covered his eyes. "Who put the lights out? Put 'em on again! Can't see where I'm going".

His friend leaned over to see what the problem was. "Don't worry, I'll see you home", he said and leaning precariously on his cane they dawdled off into the darkness.

Mouths open the girls looked at one another.

"Well, what do you think?" she looked dubiously at the café.

"Looks a bit wild, I've never heard of drunk men being thrown out of the Ashton", Julie's eyebrows met in a frown.

"Well, let's have a look through the window, that should give us a better idea".

Louisa pressed her face against the glass but no matter how much she tried she couldn't see through the rivulets of steam that slipped continuously down the pane.

"From what I can make out, it looks pretty busy in there. Odd looking customers too, not very tall, wizened faces, grey beards, pointy noses, tattoos, and 'yuk', terrible table manners. And that's just the women".

Julie bending down, rubbed her handkerchief on the glass trying to view inside the establishment from a different angle. She could see very little because the café lace held on a brass rod stretching across the bottom part of the window caused an even greater obstruction.

"Can't see anything from here. What should we do? Will we give it a go anyway?"

At that moment catching sight of a number of broomsticks in what looked like a wicker umbrella stand just outside the door Louisa, looked dubiously at the café door. The thought of joining a room full of noisy, boisterous, customers at that particular moment did not appeal to her.

"Look", she reasoned, "we could just as easily have sat in the café at home with a hot orange if that's all we're going to do. How about a wee walk now that the rain is off then we can go to the café before we catch the ferry back? Maybe by the time we return the clientele will have changed to one that's a bit better behaved".

"Could do", Julie agreed, shuddering as she looked at the contents of the stand. "So where do you suggest we walk to? It can't be too far away from the pier because we don't want to miss the return ferry".

Louisa thought hurriedly for a moment then remembering said, "Well, there is somewhere not too far from here that we could have a look at". I remember some steps I saw not far from here the last time I was in Kilcreggan. I thought they looked like they might lead somewhere interesting but I had to catch the ferry back to Gourock and didn't have time to look. How about us having a look to see where they lead to then going back to the café? Look, there they are, just over there", she pointed a finger to a dark gap between the buildings. "OK, I don't suppose a quick look will do any harm", Julie agreed.

Ten yards along from the café they found them rising out of the shadows cast by one gloomy gas lamp standing half way up.

"They don't look very inviting", Julie whispered, not at all amused when they arrived at the bottom step and she peered into the semi darkness. "Oh my goodness! What's that!" she shrieked.

A shape belonging to what appeared to belong to the large black cat that had been watching them when they arrived gave a loud "Meow", before bounding up the stair ahead of them.

"Looks like it want us to follow", Louisa decided.

Twenty five steps made from two wide rows of bricks and compacted earth rose gradually until they disappeared into what looked like woodland at the top. Rhododendron bushes towered on either side, the uppermost branches leaning over to touch the other making a canopy that shut out the moon light. Along the lower rise they could make out bare branches of viburnum, berberis, ivy and buddledja rising from a bed of brown mulched leaves. Louisa followed by Julie began to climb.

"It's a bit muddy and slippery ", said Julia, "Spooky too. 'Wooo'!" she used what she described as her 'best sepulchre voice'. Then she held out a torch its beam of light illuminating the top step.

"You brought a torch!" Louisa grinned in amazement.

"Course I did. I was a girl guide, till they threw me out. 'Be prepared' is my motto".

"Great. But don't waste it, we might be glad of it later. Oh and be careful where you put your feet and hold on to the wooden railing", Louisa called out.

Julie was right, it was rather muddy she thought as she sploshed her way up.

"I knew it, my good shoes are ruined", Julie moaned as they reached the halfway mark.

Louisa had turned around a number of times as they climbed the steps. She thought she could hear the sound of giggling and whispers coming from amongst the vegetation growing at the sides, but there was never anyone to be seen.

"Can you hear anything?" she had asked Julie.

"Just my new shoes squelching", she replied.

Arriving at the top step, relieved to be out of the claustrophobia of the bushes, they viewed what looked like a large park, flat and spacious with a few bare trees and bushes haphazardly planted at intervals.

Louisa looked around for the cat but it was nowhere to be seen.

The light from a pale moon picked out a narrow path leading towards what looked like a clump of trees in the distance.

Louisa was experiencing a growing, uncomfortable feeling about being there was beginning to wish she hadn't suggested they climb the steps. It was as if someone or something was watching them and try as she might she could not shake off the feeling.

"Have you seen enough?" she asked more than ready to turn back.

Julie considered then said, "How about us going along that path for a wee bit, it shouldn't take that long. Actually, I like it better than I thought I would. The moonlight makes it all feel sort of magical, like we're wandering in another place and time", Julie's eyes sparkled. "An adventure is entirely possible in a place like this", she waved her hand around. "What do you think? Give it another half hour then turn back?"

Although concerned Louisa didn't want to spoil her friend's enjoyment by complaining so they continued to make their way in the direction of the wooded area.

As they made their way along Louisa became aware of a chuckling sound that reminded her of a brook babbling over stones. As she tried to pinpoint from where it came, from the corner of her eye she caught sight of what appeared to be gossamer shapes sparkling and twinkling as they flickered over a little pool beside one of the low bushes. She stopped to watch.

"Why are you stopping?" Julie stopped too, "What are those?" her eyes were drawn in the same direction as Louisa's. "Oh, fairies," she whispered, "let's have a look", stepping off the path, she skipped across the grass.

"Those aren't fairies, they're more than likely fireflies", Louisa ran to catch up with her friend.

The lights disappeared by the time they reached the spot where they had been. All that was left was a shallow pool made by rain water caught in a hollow in the ground. Julie gave a disappointed sigh then her attention was caught by something else. "What on earth happened there?" she cried, pointing a finger towards a large number of worn patches in the grass on either side of the path. "Let's have a look". She ran towards one of them.

Caught up in her friend's excitement Louisa ran after her happy to indulge her imagination. As they drew closer, she exclaimed, "Why, these are faerie circles! You see, the grass is worn away by fairies dancing, and those", she pointed at the fungi, "those are toadstools where they rest during the Faerie festivities.

"Oh, yes, I've love faerie circles", excitedly Julie was caught up in the game. " Listen, I believe I can hear music. Let's join the faerie dance".

All at once Louisa remembered bedtime stories about fairies read to her when she was little.

"Stop! No!" she shouted, "it's too dangerous, we could get lost", but she was too late. Julie had impetuously stepped into the ring and disappeared from her sight.

"Julie! Julie!" She cried, "Come back!" There was no reply.

Louisa stood listening for a few moments in the hope that her friend would reappear. When she didn't Louisa thought to herself, in for a penny, in for a pound and throwing caution to the winds she stepped over the toadstools after her friend.

For a moment disoriented, Louisa found herself surrounded by a fine mist that began to slowly clear. To her surprise she found she was reclining upon what resembled a very large toadstool lazily listening to five pipers playing a merry tune. Amidst the tinkling laughter around her she remembered vaguely that she must not allow herself to slip into the enchantment that was rapidly enveloping her. This became increasingly difficult as she watched beautiful females dressed in gossamer, flower coloured dresses dancing with handsome young men in feather doublets and wishing she was one of them.

How wonderful it would be to stay here forever, she thought dreamily.

Her eyes straying from the dancers were caught by one elegant young man wearing highly-polished black leather shoes with large silver buckles, a red conical hat and a green cloak with matching pantaloons who appeared to be whispering into Julie's ear as he walked her from the dance to sit on another toadstool close to Louisa's. Julie who appeared to be listening rapturously to his words and only having eyes for the him was unaware of her friend. Louisa wanted to call her friend's name but as a contented weariness washed over her like a soft cloud, she lay back lazily watching the dancers.

With a beguiling smile Julie's companion offered her a crystal goblet of wine with a tray containing sweet meats. Eyes gazing dreamily into his Julie smiled as she thanked him.

Louisa in the process of lifting a delicious looking morsel of pink marshmallow, watched lazily as her friend raised the wine to her lips.

All at once Louisa was roughly brought back to the present when her reverie was disturbed by the yowling of a cat

Eyes flying open and fully conscious she realised with horror what she and her friend were on the cusp of doing. With all her might she threw the pink delicacy from her and swiped the goblet from Julie's hand so that it smashed into a million crystals on the hard ground.

"Don't touch that!" she screamed.

"Why did you do that?" Julie peeved, yelled amidst the silence that followed.

"Don't you realise?" Louisa cried, "we will be lost forever if we eat or drink anything while we are in a faerie circle. They will never let us go! We'll never find our way home!"

No sooner had she shouted her warning when angry screeches and cries erupted around them. Hundreds of faeries took to the air, wings whirring in anger, attacking them with tiny swords, pikes, flower petals, leaves, feathers, seed heads and little ice needles hurled into their faces assaulting them with a ferocity that caused sharp pains. The next moment a sudden gust of wind lifted each girl on high blowing them along before dropping both close to the path outside of the circle.

"Quickly! Let's get away from here", said Louisa jumping to her feet and grabbing Julie's hand.
"We're not safe", she shouted as they took to their heels together across the grass.
"What on earth happened?" Julia asked after they had outrun the angry mob and found a place to rest.

"I felt so at peace. I loved being there and wanted to stay, yet at the same time I felt I was in danger but couldn't do anything about it". She began to cry. "Oh Louisa, I'm so glad you stopped me".

"We're OK now. Best not to think about it until later", Louisa comforted her. Then tucking her arm into that of her friend they stepped back on to the path and hurried onwards.

As they walked, it occurred to Louisa how very still and silent everything was, no sign of any breeze, of rustling branches or any animal noises. Just silence.

"What was that!" Julie turned around quickly.

"What was what?" Louisa's heart jumped. "I didn't hear anything".

They stood for a few moments listening to the silence. "Imagination", Julie gave a shaky laugh.

However, as they looked back at the way they had come their attention was drawn to a low-lying, grey mist rolling over the grass behind them.

"Now where did that come from? It wasn't here a minute ago". Looking intently into it, for a moment she thought she could see the movement of tiny feet and legs.

"Something is hiding in it", Louisa found herself speaking in hushed tones.

"I'd like to turn back", Julie said, "but I don't fancy walking through that stuff".

"Well, let's go on a bit further and we might find another way".

They walked on, every now and again one of them turning around to watch the fine mist swirling at their heels. It occurred to Louisa that although it was not overtaking them it was deliberately keeping pace.

As if we are being herded into the woods, she thought. It didn't take long to reach the edge of the wood and as they stepped inside Louisa looked back once more. The cloudiness was still there, hovering a little further back. Like a sentry on guard, Louisa thought to herself.

"There might be another way back to the café through here. What do you think?", Julie asked.

"It won't do any harm to look, better than trying to retrace our steps".

They made their way through the canopy of bare branches where every now and then the moonlight glinted through making strange shadowy shapes ahead and on the bushes on either side.

Prickly, scrambling shrubs wandered across the path trying to grab an unwary foot and send the owner sprawling.

Julie shone the torch on the ground, "Watch where you put your feet", she warned, "that's the second time I've nearly tripped".

"It's awful quiet in here, You'd think there would be sounds coming from somewhere". Louisa shivered trying to throw off the growing feeling of foreboding that had been hanging over her since the mist first appeared.

"Oh, what on earth is that smell? It doesn't half pong, smells like something's died".

The stench of decay of rotted entrails and vegetation permeated the air.

Suddenly they both began to retch feeling very sick.

"We need to get out of here, quick", Louisa said beginning to feel desperate as her empty stomach attempted to regurgitate what it no longer contained. "Look, there's another path leading off from this one. Will we try it?"

"I think that has to be a good idea". Julie answered, "Maybe it will lead us out of these woods because I think I think that just might be a building bit further on and if I'm right maybe we'll find someone to ask for directions".

At that moment a cloud slipped over the moon plunging everywhere into darkness.
Julie, thanking her lucky stars that she had thought to bring the torch, switched it on

Squinting her eyes "Yes, you could be right, that might be a wall", Louisa said looking towards the shape. Encouraged they made their way towards it and soon found themselves on the far side of the woods looking on to an open space.

Setting out to cross it, the firm ground soon gave way to high reeds and the soggy water-logged soil of marshy ground. Walking became difficult, one minute bouncing unsteadily on springy moss, the other sinking up to their ankles in dark peaty water.

Louisa cast her eyes around hoping to find a more substantial surface, "That looks like a path", she said pointing towards what appeared to be a narrow raised mossy area formed from the trunks of many trees that had been felled many decades ago before being laid end to end to make a sort of bridge and proving a more stable surface.

Making their way towards it and testing it with her foot Julie decided it was firm enough to bear their weight.

"Not as good as a pavement but it will do fine", she said. Walking carefully along the slippery moss-covered surface they reached firmer ground leading to a high, dry-stone wall.

"Can you see a gate?" Louisa whispered.

Julie shone the beam from the torch back and forth across the surface but all that they could make out was more wall.

"I suppose if we feel our way around it we'll find one eventually" she decided.

After searching for a while without success Louisa said, "I'm beginning to think there isn't one".

"There's bound to be a gate," Julie answered, "How would anyone get in or out without one. There's no point in building a wall without a gate".

She made her way around it a little further, "Over here!" Louisa heard her call, "I've found a step".

When Louisa reached her she was standing almost halfway up the wall "Let's climb over, we can find the gate from inside when we want to leave. Can you give me a punt up?"

Louisa saw that Julie stood on a large rock sticking out at the bottom of the wall. Stretching up she was trying to get a grip on some of the stones on top.

"Careful, there might be glass up there", warned Louisa, hoping Julie would change her mind.

"It's OK, I've found a foothold. I'm nearly there", her friend, called heaving herself upwards.

Successfully straddling the top of the wall Julie held the torch beam under her chin.

"Wooo! Spooky!" then suddenly she screamed,

"Oh… No o o!" and disappeared from sight.

"Are you OK?" Louisa shouted, but there was no reply.

"Oh hell!" she thought, "That could be quite a drop on the other side. Maybe she's broken her neck".

She began to call quietly, "Julie, Julie, are you all right?" Still there was no reply.

All at once her nostrils were assaulted by a smell of rotted fish. Then she had a feeling that someone or something had crept up behind her and was breathing into her ear. As the hairs on the back of her neck began to prickle. she turned around quickly. At first she thought there was nothing there then as her eyes became more accustomed to the dark, she saw a crouched figure of about four foot high, covered in shaggy hair running fast then without warning disappearing into what appeared to be a hole in the ground and she heard a snort of unpleasant laughter coming from out of the darkness.

CHAPTER 3

"Julie!" she cried again, "Where are you?"

"I'm OK", a voice answered from the other side of the wall.

The cloud that had been covering the moon chose that moment to move on and once more the place was bathed in a cold, pale glow.

"Oh! You should see this", Julie's voice was filled with wonder.

In no time, glad to get away from the marshland as well as whatever was inhabiting it, Louisa had scrambled up and was sitting on top of the wall, legs dangling, gazing at the silhouette of a large turreted building set amongst spacious grounds.

"It looks like a castle ", she said forgetting about the scare she had just had. "Will we have a look at it?" she asked. "What do you think?"

"Come on", Julie decided, "Let's have a look. Maybe somebody can tell us how to get back to the road".

Dropping off the wall to join Julie, Louisa looked around.

The vegetation was quite long and unkempt. Still convinced that she could hear whispering and quiet laughter from where the grass grew longest, she moved it aside looking in all directions for the source. But whenever she reached the spot she was sure the sound was coming from, all fell silent and giggling would break out in a different place. Eventually tiring of the game Louisa waded through beds of nettles scattered amongst the knee-high, wet grass. Giving a groan of pain she hurriedly grabbed for a handful of dock leaves that were growing nearby and began to rub them on the stings until the pain eased.

Searching to find a path she picked her way towards some yew trees then bumped her knee against a piece of stone, its ornate top just showing above the greenery. What's this? she wondered placing her hand on it to give it a shake before finding it was firmly anchored to the ground.

Brushing the grass aside to get a better look, it occurred to her how cold it felt. "It's marble", she thought sliding her hands over the exterior. One side was smooth but her fingers felt markings engraved into the surface of the other. Moving to the other side she bent down to see if she could read them out but there wasn't enough light. She did however make out the letters. Feeling with her fingers she read out, "P, something, L, something, PPE, then something, R, E, T, something, N. Someone's name no doubt, but doesn't make any sense".

Then realising where they were, "Careful", she called out to Julie, "I think we might be in the middle of a cemetery".

After taking a few minutes to look around she said, "It's not a very big one, only about four tombstones that I can see. Come on let's have a look at the castle to see if it's worth another visit in daylight then we'll go back to the cafe".

When they found their way to a cobbled path, they were relieved to get out of the wet grass.

Without warning an owl hooted. Startled, Louisa looked up to see a white owl swooping low as it made its way slowly across the ground towards some trees.

The path led them to wide steps leading down to formal gardens, the moonlight picking out the symmetrical layout of clipped hedges, topiaries of yew and box and beds of pruned rose plants.

The girls stood looking at the expanse before them.

"Oh", whispered Louisa. "I know this place", as an icy feeling of familiarity struck her. There was something, just on the brink of her memory. Just as she almost grasped it, Julie spoke and it was gone.

"I never expected anything like this It must belong to the castle, it's fantastic. Can you make out what that square shape in the grass is? Julie asked. "Look, that square with the large figures standing on it?"

Louisa looked towards it then smiled. "I know what that is. Let's walk over".

They walked across the grass, silvery in the moonlight.

"Look at the height of those", said Julie, "they look like figures carved from tree trunks. The tallest one has to be about six feet high. Looks a bit spooky from here. I don't know if I like the look of it".

"It isn't spooky, can't you see? It's a giant game of chess", Louisa laughed. "My Dad has a chess board. A lot smaller than this one. He taught me to play when I was twelve".

"Chess? I've heard of chess but I don't know anything about it". Julie stared at the huge wooden figures lined up in two rows at each end of the chequered board. "Gross! What's it about and what on earth are those supposed to be?" Julie pointed towards the pieces.

"Those are pieces, you use those to play the game. It's a game of strategy for two players. The aim is to capture the king. When the king has nowhere left to go the game is lost. Each piece has its own rules and moves differently in certain directions".

She pointed a finger. Each player has two rooks – they are the ones that look like castles, two bishops, two knights, one king, one queen and eight pawns".

"Looks like an odd sort of game to me", Julie frowned. By this time they were standing on the edge of the large stone square.

Julie stepped onto the square making her way towards one of the rooks. What's it made of? Feels like wood", she said stroking the rounded head of a pawn in front of it..

"Let's try to move one of these", Julie said, squeezing between two pawns. When she was behind one of them she tried to push it forward. Nothing happened. "Well let's try this", she said and leaning her back against the pawn she walked her feet up the front of the rook. "Not much room here", she grunted trying to straighten her legs.

Although pushing with all her might, nothing happened at first until there was a slight creaking sound that grew gradually into a tremendous grating noise as the pawn moved slowly forward two spaces leaving Julie lying on her back between the two pieces.

Louisa's hand flew to her mouth as she looked around. She was sure someone must have heard them.

Helping Julie to her feet. "Are you hurt?" she asked her. "Ooh! Bit of a bump", she moaned rubbing her bottom, "bound to bruise but I'll be OK", she said as they stood listening. "There's nobody around or they would have been here by now. Let's have a look at the rest".

She walked backwards to the middle of the board trying to get a better view of the pieces.

"The tallest one in the middle of the line", she took a step back to look at it. "Don't tell me, that's a king and that's got to be the queen standing beside him.

"I'm getting hungry", Louisa moaned rubbing her stomach.

"OK we'll go back now but got to give the king a wee kiss".

She skipped over to the king climbing on top of the pawn in front. Stretching her arms she wrapped them around the neck planting a loud kiss on lips which, to her surprise, were soft and warm.

Suddenly there was clap of thunder accompanied by a loud shriek of anger that appeared to come from the queen as the chess board began to spin. Louisa fell to the ground while Julie, tossed from the king, landed a little further away. Both clung on as best they could as the board rotated faster and faster.

"I can't hold on any longer ", shrieked Julie as she began sliding across the board towards the grass.

Louisa watched in horror as a flash of lightning lit up the sky and Julie skidding across the board before disappearing from her sight. A second flash saw herself also sliding with speed towards the edge and thrown onto some grass.

Julie was nowhere to be seen.

Dazed, she sat there trying to get her bearings. It was no longer dark and she could see sunlight attempting to penetrate the smoky haze that hung in the air.

Suddenly she heard men shouting. When she looked around she was aghast to see foot soldiers running in her direction.

Behind them came charging cavalry wearing thick tunics with iron gauntlets and helmets. Their broadswords glinting in the sunlight as roaring like demons from hell they gained on them.

All at once she felt someone grab her by the arm and she too was running, running for her life with the retreating men towards the shelter of trees in the distance. Her feet hardly seemed to be touching the ground as she flew along when suddenly, without warning her rescuer stopped. He dropped his sword, arched his back then dropping to his knees fell forward to lie face down in the churned-up mud, a dagger sticking from his back. Giving great dry sobs she dragged herself towards the stricken man to see what she could do to help him.

As she got closer, she saw what to her looked like two insubstantial veil like structures on each shoulder blade. They shimmered as they almost lifted and opened but unsuccessful, grey and lifeless they collapsed onto his back again. Her would be rescuer turned his head as she reached him, "Run lass", he gasped, before the light left his eyes and she saw that he was dead.

Struggling to regain her feet she realised the elastic on the waist of her petticoat must have broken so that the material had slipped to entangle her legs and feet.

She could now smell the heat and sweat off the fast approaching, merciless enemy as they gained on the stragglers. Rapidly travelling over the terrain as they got closer, she was struck with the fact of how closely they resembled one another. Huge brutish beasts, beady black malevolent eyes on each side of a dripping snout astride plunging forward on snarling, chain-mailed beasts.

The leader, its lips drawn back to show teeth that had been filed into sharp points made disjointed grunting noises as it rode down on her determined to finish the job.

CHAPTER 4

Reaching out to grasp the abandoned sword, Louisa raised the blade flat across her head preparing to protect herself. The snarling man dismounted, and reaching her he bent down to wrenched the blade of the dagger from the dead man's back, licking it first he wiped it on his tunic and replaced it in a sheath at his side.

As if savouring the moment, he stood examining Louisa with his cold, unblinking eyes.

Withdrawing the sword from its sheath, he raised the blade aloft. As it glinted in the rays of the sun he paused as if considering the best angle from which to deliver the blow.

With a laugh, almost playfully, he flattened the blade, drew it back then brought it forward with speed giving her a vicious swipe on her side. Screaming in agony the strength in her arm gone she dropped the sword down in front of her. Unexpectedly, a sudden blazing anger leant her strength and using her uninjured arm to take the weight she lifted the sword unsteadily in front of her. The enemy gave a disdainful snigger then as if tired of the game, he lifted the sword on high preparing to deliver the fatal blow.

Sick with fear and disbelief, she closed her eyes waiting for death.

The blow never came. Without warning her assailant give an intake of breath and a muttered curse. Opening her eyes she saw his sword had fallen from his hand. His teeth were clenched as he attempted to stretch a hand far enough over his shoulder to grasp at a dagger embedded in his back.

The enemy pursuers began scattering as a knight, sword in hand, his fine gleaming cloak streaming out behind him as he lashed out from one side to the other, bore down on them clearing a passageway towards her.

As she got her knees she felt an arm reach down to catch her around her waist lifting her on high as they galloped towards the wood. Almost there, the horse suddenly sailed into the air leaping over a large concealed trench that had been dug in the soft earth along the front and forward on each side for several yards. As they traversed the ditch Louisa saw what looked like hundreds of leather helmeted heads concealed below.

When the retreating soldiers reached the front of the ditch they stopped then turned to face the roaring, oncoming attackers. All at once, powerful wings opened on each warrior's shoulders lifting them on high carrying them behind the approaching enemy.

At the same time hundreds of their concealed, armed compatriots emerged armed with pike and halberd roaring great battle cries as they prepared to engage the outflanked the foe. Behind these, longbow men emerged from the wood. The fore runners of the opposing army, realising they had been lured into a trap tried to rein in their mounts with little success. Dismounting, swords in hand they attempted to prepare themselves as the pike men advanced.

Once across the ditch her rescuer trotted into the woods gently setting her down beside the stump of an old tree. Lifting his visor he said softly, "Rest here my lady until I return".

Wishing her farewell and wheeling his horse around he turned towards the noise of battle to resume the fight.

For a while Louisa sat silently aware only of the excruciating pain in her side and trying to find a position that would alleviate it. Slowly, as she began to recover her wits she looked around. What had happened? Where was she? Her feet felt cold, wet and uncomfortable. When she leaned forward to remove the soft mud from shoes, her arm moved and the pain that shot down to her hand and across her chest was so severe that she fainted.

Not knowing how long she had been unconscious when she recovered, she found herself lying against the stump of the tree in the soft green grass listening to the sounds of battle. A great cacophony of human voices roaring out their battle cries, metal clashing, men shouting, screams of pain rent the air then suddenly, all was silent.

Louisa had lost all sense of time as she sat listening to the silence when her ears pricked up to catch an eerie, metallic clinking sound softly making its way in her direction.
Looking around for something with which to defend herself, she found a sturdy branch with a point at the end

beside her. Holding it in one hand she prepared to jab an approaching enemy.

As she waited, heart in her mouth, a tall figure in chain mail appeared from amongst the trees. Helmet in hand his brown hair tousled, he approached her then stopped to gaze at the serious looking, unkempt little warrior staring up at him.

"Demoiselle", he bowed, Je ne suis pas ton ennemi. C'est moi qui vous ai amene a endroit. Dis-moi, comment se fait-il que tu sois dans ces regions? Ou est votre maisonSes yeux sombre sourirent dans les siens. Oh, permettez-moi de me presenter. Je suis Philuppe Breton

She was swamped in relief when she recognised his voice, it was the knight who had rescued her. He had come back. He's speaking French, she decided.

"Je ne parle pas francais monsieur", she answered, "I do not speak French",

He smiled, "Ah, you speak English?"

"I am not your enemy. It was I who brought you to this place. Tell me, how come you to be in these parts? Where is your home?" His dark eyes smiled down into hers. "Oh, please allow me to present myself. I am Philippe Breton.

"Yes, I do", she answered.

He repeated his question in English, "How come you to be here today?"

Louisa's senses began to swim once more, "I don't know", she said before falling backwards into darkness.

"Ah no! You are ill", concerned, he dropped to his knees by her side, "you have been injured", he said when she gave a cry trying to support the arm on the injured side with her hand. "Come, I will take you to my sister".

She felt herself lifted gently from the ground and heard the gentle wafting of wings as she slowly and smoothly moved through the air and both she and the knight descended onto horseback.

With a gentle flick of reins the knight's horse moved off. Barely conscious, Louisa was aware only of the regular rhythm of the horse as she was held against the chest of the knight.

In time, she didn't know how long it took, they came to a halt and she felt herself being slowly lifted down, his arms cradling her as he shouted instructions to shadowy figures waiting to greet him.

"Poor dear", she heard a female voice, "This way".
"Julie?" she asked, but there was no reply.

For some time afterward, it might have been days or weeks, she drifted in and out of consciousness. She was vaguely aware of being gently bathed, poultices applied to her injuries, dressed in soft cotton nightgowns and after taking a few spoonful's of bread steeped in warm milk and something wonderful, of drifting into a deep sleep to dream of faerie beings fluttering lovingly around her.

As time passed and she came slowly out of her delirium she became aware of one young woman, a constant companion, flitting in and out of the room, sitting by her bed singing lullabies or speaking softly to her as she brushed her hair.

On other nights she was aware of a tall, thin figure with pointed ears, its eyes, shards of icy glass, watching over her.

But clearest of all was the tender voice of the knight speaking tenderly and wiping her brow.

Time passed and as her wounds began to heal and her strength returned, she remembered a different life and place outside of the world in which she now existed. Her one thought was I have to find my way home.".

One morning as she sat thinking how very strange everything was, her thoughts were interrupted by the sweet voice she had come to recognise.

"Julie?" she asked hopefully.

"No, I am Ellyn, the sister of Philippe. My dear, we have been so worried about you but thank the Lord you are now recovering".

"Please, Ellyn, can you tell me where I am? I am so confused. I don't know if I am awake or dreaming most of the time. I don't know what to believe.

"Oh, my dear", said Ellyn, "You are in the Land of Fae. You were severely injured when my brother found you and brought you here".

When Ellyn continued to say they had not been aware that mortals were involved in the war, Louisa was surprised.

She told her that she'd had no idea there was a land of Fae much less of a war taking place there. How she arrived there was a complete mystery and apart from being rescued she remember little else apart from knowing she had to find her way home.

Ellyn said gently, "Please don't worry. We will take care of you until you are well enough to leave. After you bathe would you feel strong enough to allow Philippe to carry you downstairs to sit awhile?"

"Oh yes thank you, that would be nice", Louisa breathed. "It's time I tried to get back to normal".

"The fresh air will help you to feel better I am sure", Louisa watched Ellyn making her way to the nightstand admiring the glistening, cobwebby veil hanging from her shoulders.

Holding the mirror handed to her by Ellyn, Louisa was shocked when she saw at the grey-eyed, pale girl gazing back at her. She hardly recognised herself. How long have I been ill? she wondered. How would her family or friends recognise her now.

As Ellyn wrapped a shawl around her shoulders Louisa was aware of a 'purring' sound and a large black cat, pointed face and ears with a pure white spot in the middle of his chest jumped onto the chair beside her. "That's Siddi, he has been watching over you during the night", Ellyn told her as she stroked the cats large head.

As she called to her brother, Philippe who had been hovering outside of the door entered the room greeting Louisa with a smile then lifting her into his arms he smoothly moving towards the bedroom door.

I feel as if I'm flying, Louisa thought to herself before catching her breath when she became aware of the two wings extending from Philippe's shoulders.

Gliding along a corridor Louisa saw standards and a coat of arms on the wall. She just had time to notice an azure blue shield with a large white feather on each side of a cross, and above that a knight's helmet with a white owl atop the crest.

When they reached a wide flight of stairs they began to descend, floating upon the fragrant air.

Making their way to a settle his wings folded behind his back as he made her comfortable amongst the soft cushions and animal skins before seating himself on the sweetly smelling rushes beside her.

Thanking him, Louisa smiled at the charming young man. He looked around twenty years of age, tall and upright with deep brown, smiling eyes and a shock of dark curly hair. He told Louisa how much he looked forward to showing her around the grounds when she felt well enough.

Her senses were bathed in the perfume issuing from sweet scented rushes covering the floor and the jugs of dried rosemary and lavender scattered around the room. She looked about her at the whitewashed walls festooned with deep blue hangings and the most beautiful embroideries.

Ellyn's pale cheeks took on a rosy hue as Louisa admired them telling her how beautiful she thought they were.

"How I wish I could sew like that", she said wistfully.

Ellyn's blush deepened. "I would be more than happy to show you how if you wish. These are my work", she explained.

For the next half an hour she showed Louisa the threads and some of the different stitches she used.

After the midday meal Philippe sat talking with her, telling her a little about his and Ellyn's lives. He and his sister were twins, devoted to one another. As he spoke Louisa noticed that he and his sister shared the same kind of lopsided grin when they were amused.

He explained that this was his family home but when they had been orphaned at a young age they were taken into the care of a guardian until he reached his majority and came into his inheritance.

His family had served the monarchy for nigh on three hundred years, the last four generations fighting by the king's side.

In return, Louisa told him what little she remembered about her life and how differed her world was from his.

As the days passed Louisa found that she and Philippe were spending more and more time in each other's company. She was happy to be with him especially enjoying his gentle sense of humour.

Although she knew he was a seasoned warrior he never spoke about his part in the service of king in the faraway. But Ellyn had confided in Louisa that what he experienced during those times had sickened him but although many nobles could choose to pay proxies to serve in their stead, Philippe felt it was his duty to fight alongside his men.

As her health improved Louisa became so involved in the daily life of the beautiful manor house that finding her way home became less important.

She enjoyed attending a daily service with Philippe and Ellyn before breakfast and meeting the many disparate callers who came to visit each day.

Siddi who was never far from her side appeared to take exception to some of the ladies, especially those whose wings took on a bright pinkish hue and never missed a chance to flutter them coquettishly whenever Philippe was around.

One in particular, whose habit it was to roughly move him aside with her foot always received the noisiest of hisses when she came close.

CHAPTER 5

Louisa deciding it would be wise to learn more about the strange world in which she now found herself,
encouraged Ellyn to tell her about her life and the times in which she lived.

When she told her about the secret underground tunnels she and Philippe had found when they were children and some of their adventures amongst them, Louisa pricked up her ears.

The tunnels led past a mine from which dwarfs dug precious stones and minerals. They had been added as a means of escape in the event of siege.

Stretching for a distance under the mansion they provided a means of eluding an enemy via the sea. As it had been many years since she had been in them Ellyn decided she would like to go there again and wondered if Louisa would care to explore them with her.

When Louisa enthusiastically agreed they arranged to set out after the midday meal.

The sun that had been shining brightly all morning was covered in cloud by the end of the midday meal. Both wearing warm shawls and stout boots and accompanied by Siddi made their way to the basement and from there down dank, musty steps leading to a curtained door which creaked and groaned slowly open when they both pushed against it.

As soon as they entered Louisa was aware of a vibration coming from under her feet, accompanied by a low, rhythmic bumping sound.

"It's coming from the mine", Ellyn explained, "we can't hear it in the rest of the house".

A corridor bathed in a greenish glow issuing from the walls stretched before them. Must be phosphorous, Louisa thought.

After walking fifty yards along it they came upon the gate to a mine shaft beside a steep cliff face at what appeared to be the end of the tunnel. However, hidden from view and a little further on it was possible to make one's way through an opening in the rock leading to a number of narrower passages branching off from another main one.

Siddi danced before them towards one of the passages. Following him, Louisa was amazed to find herself in a sizable chamber, its walls and roof issuing a myriad of shimmering, twinkling lights. Ellyn's gossamer wings unfolding, opened wide in pleasure.

"This is the most beautiful of all", Ellyn whispered.

Louisa gazed in wonder at the jewel colours of crystals and gem stones glinting in the surface of the walls, their beauty enhanced by little blades of light filtering downwards from some outside source.

"This has always been my favourite", Ellyn told Louisa. "It doesn't lead anywhere but it is so pretty".

Retracing their steps to the main corridor Ellyn pointed out another a less noticeable fork a little further on.

"This leads outside. There is a little stream at the end which can grow to a raging torrent when it rains heavily". Siddi, giving little hissing sounds, followed reluctantly behind them.

"He doesn't like water", Ellyn explained.

Louisa could smell the dampness and mould as they made their way carefully along the rough, cold, narrow

passage towards what looked like daylight at the far end.
Ellyn pointed towards two little boats made from a
framework of willow covered in animal skins tied up to
iron rings in the wall. "One of the labourers on the estate
looks after these. Remember they are here, one day you
might be glad of them".

Louisa gave an involuntary shiver. She had a growing
feeling that something unpleasant was hiding and had
been watching them.

She was relieved when Ellyn said, "Oh dear, I think you
have been here long enough and it is cold. Time to go
back and I'll tell you a little more of our adventures
where it is warmer".

Hurriedly they retraced their steps and were soon back at
the main hall. When they settled down and were warm
once more, Ellyn spoke a little more about the passages.
In turn she was just as keen to learn about Louisa's
world encouraging her to share her memories as they
began to emerge.

She didn't know what to make of them, asking herself if
they were merely the stuff of dreams or if Louisa come
from an extraordinary world, a much more powerful

magical world than hers, existing beyond the bounds of reality.

Ellyn gasped not only with delight when Louisa described ships that could move without the need of sail, wind or human energy.

A few days after their visit to the tunnels as they sat quietly in the garden enjoying the sound of the bees buzzing amongst the flowers and watching the butterflies in graceful flight Ellyn said quietly, "Louisa, I love to listen to stories about your mortal life, and wonder if you remember any more about how you entered the land of Fae?"

Louisa thought for a moment, "Much of it is unclear but what I do remember is my dearest friend Julie and I looking at a chess board with enormous chess pieces, the board began to rotate, my friend was thrown off and I was caught up amongst fleeing soldiers and Philippe rescued me.

When she went on to describe how she received her injuries Ellyn was horrified,

"The brute!" she exclaimed and all at once her wings began to expand, trembling with agitation before slowly settling back once more.

I keep forgetting that Ellyn is a faerie, a beautiful faerie, Louisa thought to herself.

As the days passed her mind slowly unveiled more memories and she was able to describe what had happened as they crossed the stormy sea. She told Ellen about the kelpies, great horses unshod and unbridled rising above the waves and the blue men demanding the captain of their little boat complete the verse of a strange sounding poem or drown with everyone onboard.

"And your friend was unaware of this?" Ellyn looked thoughtful.

"Is there anyone in your family who is aware of happenings that others are not?"

"Well, perhaps my mother. It was thought that she had second sight but she always denied it and would not allow us to speak of it".

"Ah!" Ellyn smiled, "That explains much".

She did not say anything further about it but went on to ask Louisa to tell her more about her adventures.

They spoke late into the night, Ellyn laughing helplessly as she described the inebriated customers from the café - after Louisa explained what a café was.

Ellyn looked worried when she spoke about finding the faerie rings and how they both entered one of them.
"It was as if we were both enchanted", Louisa tried to explain. "We knew if we ate or drank anything while we were there we could be trapped forever, but in a way that didn't seem to matter".
For an instant she stopped speaking as a frown creased her forehead.
Ellyn, aware of what she was thinking assured her,
"No, my dear that would never happen here. You are welcome to remain or leave as long as you wish. Our tribe does not use magic to detain mortals".
Louisa reassured, spoke as if thinking aloud, "In my time no one really believes in magic or faeries any more", she said sadly.

"If I was to tell anyone about being here I would be locked away in a mad house unless I admitted I was lying.

The general we believe that everything that happens has a logical explanation. But when I think about what has happened to me, I know that there is more to it and our different worlds must exist side by side. I don't really know how or why I arrived here. I'm just here.

After sitting quietly thinking for a while Ellyn said, "I believe that you are meant to be with Philippe and me. But let's not worry about it for a while. Things have a way of working themselves out.

Their friendship grew as they came to know one another better. As the days passed Louisa thought how so very often time itself seemed strange. The here and now was not in doubt but the rest was becoming a hazy memory. Her clearest memories were of a little girl and a teenager living by the sea in Scotland with her parents, of going to school, of close friendships especially with Julia of whom Ellyn reminded her.

Other more shadowy substances lingered but she could not really describe them as memories.

It surely was not possible to have memories of the future, but might they be instances of the second-sight her mother had spoken of. Every so often when she was alone she allowed herself to drift, and in this state dreamlike memories descended, so slowly at first then faster and faster like vast clouds of snowflakes enveloping her in drifts from which she had to fight her way out. There was a marriage - an unhappy one which she quickly dismissed from her mind. Then there was the factory and a university, but clearest of all amongst these was the memory of a man, a man of the past, the present, the future, the memory of whom filled her heart with joy.

When the weather was mild they sat in the garden talking and laughing together. Ellyn delighted in Louisa's company finding her strange sense of humour appealing. She had never met anyone like Louisa before. At times she thought she could be quite mad especially as she entertained her with exciting stories about her home and times.

What a wonderful magical world Louisa came from, Ellyn thought.

She was amazed by the description of small square boxes from which came the sound minstrels playing, of men, women, and children singing or telling tales, of men with serious voices speaking of battles in far-away lands. "How on earth could one man squeeze into a little box sitting upon a table let alone many people at the same time?" she laughed. When Louisa tried to explain about sounds carried by waves that could not be seen she shrieked with delight arguing that of course everyone could see waves when they looked at the sea.

Open mouthed she listened as Louisa tried to explain that although her people did not have wings, they could still fly by getting into the stomach of a large metal bird or collapsing in laughter as Louisa told her about a visit to the cinema people where people met in a large room to view different men and women in moving portraits having adventures.

As Siddi sat beside them listening, the look on his face gave Louisa the distinct impression that the cat understood everything she spoke about perfectly.

Ellyn in turn confided in Louisa how her parents and another noble family had arranged a betrothal between her and their son when they were babies.
Her groom to be had died in battle three years earlier and she was still a maiden. One year later she was betrothed to a naval officer who had gone down with his ship in a sea battle before they could marry. Since then she had given serious consideration to life in a monastic order but wasn't so sure this was the right direction for her. Now, there was another older man named Henry, Lord of Elveshome, a friend of Philippe's was paying her court. Although he was a bit older she was giving his wishes consideration.
Louisa was shocked. Ellyn couldn't have been more than one year older than her yet she had been betrothed twice and now almost again.
"But what about love?" Louisa had asked her, "Surely you wouldn't marry a man you didn't love?"

Ellyn, surprised, stared at her, "Marry for love? We don't marry for love. Our marriages are arranged for many reasons but never love, Although sometimes…", her words tailed off while she examined her embroidery for a few minutes, as if considering the idea.

Changing the subject she said, "Oh please, tell me more about how you learned to ride your horse… no, bycisil, bycle, you know what I mean, it is so funny".

Allowing her to change the subject, Louisa went on to describe penny farthings, tricycles and, yet again, her attempts to learn to ride a bicycle as Ellyn sat with her lips moving retelling the loved story with her friend.

CHAPTER 6

Louisa had been a little taken aback when she was invited to join Ellyn in weapons practice each morning. Ellyn, seeing the look of surprise on her face had asked, "Who do you suppose helps to defend town and castle when the able bodied men are away fighting?"

Louisa hadn't given this much consideration before. She had supposed she was now living in a time that existed centuries before that of her world. Her idea of women in the middle ages had been gained from history books and from the cinema where all women were portrayed as subservient, docile, weak and often rather brainless.

Of course, when she thought about it, women had to be resilient and tough and what women would not fight using any weapon in her means to protect those she loved.

When she enthusiastically agreed to join Ellyn, she was provided with the appropriate wear and was introduced to the use of the longsword and spears as well as arbalest practice on the archery range.

One morning after instructing them Philippe, searched out Louisa. He told her how much of a difference she had made to his and his sister's lives. It had been such a long time since he heard Ellyn laugh so much, she had known such sadness and there had not been much to laugh about. He had so many demands on his time between running the estate and the service of the king he could not give her the companionship she needed. Louisa was aware that his time was much in demand, his mornings taken up by inspecting his estate, attending business matters relating to his land, political discussions and decisions, judicial responsibilities, weapons practise before mid-morning prayers and the mid-day meal.

He told Louisa that he realised that she herself was sometimes homesick but if she would bring herself to remain awhile as a companion and sometimes chaperone to his sister it would make them both happy. Louisa thought that Ellyn had probably told her brother about her past life but he never questioned her and for that she was grateful.

"Our parents died when we were children", he continued. "Although we were taken into the care of our guardians I was her big brother and was mindful as such that it was my duty not only to keep her safe but happy. She has been in need of intelligent female companionship, which has been absent until you came to live with us.".

Philippe went on to admit to the added worry of fortune hunters, more often than not wastrel brothers of at least two of the women who hung around the house trying to ingratiate themselves, taking advantage of her loneliness when he was abroad on the king's service. Although Ellyn had a mind of her own and could defend herself he felt that Louisa would be more than capable of helping her ward off unwelcome advances until she came to a decision about her future.

Louisa smiled, telling Philippe she would be more than happy to remain with Ellyn who had taken such good care of her. She had grown to love her like a sister and had been hoping to find some small way of returning their kindness. Perhaps this could be the answer.

Philippe, rising to his feet smiling thanked her. As he walked towards the door he turned around to look at her. "Louisa", he said, "I ask you to stay not only for Ellyn's sake. She is not the only one who needs you".

Later, when Louisa sat pondering on Philippe's words, she conceded that the longer she stayed the more difficult it would be to leave when the time came, It was true that she had come to love Ellyn as a sister, but Philippe, what about Philippe? For the first time she admitted to herself that every time she looked up to find his eyes on her she felt gentle bumping in her heart and the growing affection when she thought about him before falling asleep each night.

When they all sat together in the candle-lit lantern stillness of the garden in the company of Philippe's friends that evening, Louisa was struck by the silence. She enjoyed the peace. It was all so different from the life she was used to. Here she wasn't bombarded with background noise. No television or juke boxes blaring away, no sound of trains, buses or cars, no machinery.

Folk relied on themselves and animals to produce the food and goods needed to live.

When a dog barked or someone shouted or dropped something heavy the noise was heard with greater intensity than it would at home.

What she did not enjoy was the darkness. In the dark, nights had a different kind of quality, one tinged with apprehension.

Shadows, faces, unexpected figures suddenly appearing, a quiet tread, were picked up with an intense awareness and a readiness to defend oneself or run.

She came out of her reverie when she heard Ellyn's voice ask, "Louisa, would you like to accompany me into town tomorrow morning, I think you are strong enough now?"

"The town? Oh yes, I would enjoy that" Louisa said feeling quite excited.

The following day Louisa found a riding habit waiting for her in her dressing room. Ellyn helped her to get into it after breakfast admiring the finished effect.

She found a pretty palfrey beside Ellyn's waiting for her in the main drive.

Ellyn mounted while Louisa was assisted to the saddle. Accompanied by one of the groomsman riding discretely behind she gingerly flicked the reins and set off. The track was uneven and rough. Louisa was relieved she was on horseback which although difficult was preferable to being bumped about inside a coach.

As they approached the town Louisa put her hand over her mouth in horror, shocked by the sight of a hanged man swinging from a gibbet at the entrance to the town his wings no more than skeletal. Ellyn who did not appear to be at all dismayed paid it no more attention that she would have the branch of a tree.

On reaching the church a cloaked figure, hood pulled well forward over his face sat on the steps rattling a begging bowl. Most of the townsfolk gave him a wide berth but Ellyn signalled to the groomsman who threw a few coins into it.

As Louisa watched a bandaged hand, most of the fingers rotted away, appeared out of the cloak. attempting to grasp the coins she gasped.

"Come away my dear, let us visit the market", Ellyn whispered when she saw the look of horror on her face. "What's the matter with that poor man?| Louisa gasped. "Why he's a leper. Are there no lepers in your country?" Ellyn looked surprised when she replied, "No, from what I know, there haven't been any cases reported for two hundred years and now the disease can be treated with antibiotics, leprosy will be wiped out all over the world".

Ellyn was just going to ask what 'antibiotic' meant when she was distracted by the groomsman signalling that they had reached their destination.
Once they dismounted the groomsman took charge of their mounts arranging for provision of water and oats before following the ladies at a discreet distance. Louisa had been surprised to find that riding side saddle felt much more comfortable and safer than she thought it would be and was quite please when she realised how much she was enjoying it especially when this was the first time for her.
When Ellyn reminded Louisa to protect her script as cutpurses abounded she tucked it under her skirt.

The market was noisy, colourful and smelly, body odour mingled with that of spices, oils and strong perfumes. Unwashed townsfolk pushed and jostled one another for a good view watching jugglers, acrobats and fire eaters performed at one side of the square while mummers performed at the other.

While they admired the silks and lace on one of the stalls, a gushing female voice said, "Ellyn, my dearest Ellyn, how are you? You have been so busy of late. How is Philippe? It is such a long time since I have seen him. He always seems to be away from home when I call."

To Louisa's surprise she heard Ellyn try to stifle a snort by turning it into a cough.

The voice belonged to the woman Louisa had noticed as a regular visitor accompanied by two handsome young men and another woman.

Apart from looking down her aristocratic nose, the woman, Lady Annabella du Burr, barely acknowledged Louisa when Ellen presented her.

Ellyn, annoyed, brought the conversation politely to an end and taking Louisa's arm wished the woman a good day while she went on to admire the little birds in the cages at the next stall.

That evening, tired and happy, they returned home to examined the treasures they had purchased and regale Philippe with stories about the sights they had seen.

Philippe for his part had two pieces of news, the first one was he would accompany Calbot, Earl of Flamsbury to Gasomny in the near future and secondly he planned a feast in the grand hall with dancing afterwards.

The thought of a feast and dancing delighted Louisa but she worried about the types of dances they would do, sure she would not be familiar with any of them. When she confided in Ellyn, she was assured that she and Philippe would teach her some steps.

After listening to her brother's news Ellyn appeared rather preoccupied. Concerned, Louisa asked her friend if there was something troubling her.

"Oh", she said, "my brother is worried should anything happen to him I would be unprotected. I think he will formally present a possible suitor, his friend I told you about. Oh, don't look so horrified my dear Louisa", she smiled when she saw the look on Louisa's face, "he would never force me to do anything against my will. But come, let us not dwell on this matter, allow me to show you a dance you might enjoy".

They joined Philippe in the great hall where he sat beside an enormous fireplace, the apple logs sparking and sizzling as he listened to a group of travelling minstrels filling the air with the music from pipe and tabor, cittern and shawm.

Ellyn knelt by his knee, "Philippe, my dear", she said, "I wish to show Louisa how to dance the lavolta. She would like to learn. Would you help me show her the steps?".

Philippe gave her a questioning look but when he caught sight of Louisa's worried face he smiled. "Of course sister. Take my hand. We will demonstrate", he smiled to Louisa,

"Louisa, there are only a few steps to remember, watch us first".

Giving a nod to the minstrels, he called, "Lavolta!" and the musicians began to play.

As the music began, Philippe and Ellyn side by side, her hand in his and gazing into one another's eyes, walked into the centre of the room. After bowing to one another, they joined hands once more and picking up the rhythm of the music each brushed the right foot forward hopping and setting it down in front and following with a kick. They repeated this with the left foot and when both feet met they lifted both heels and paused. This was the first step which the repeated a number of times.

Louisa was just getting the idea when suddenly Philippe place a hand on Ellyn's back and the other below her left breast while she placed her arms over his shoulders and with a kick, hop, step, kick, he lifted her high in the air as if she was as light as thistledown before setting her down again. Louisa gasped as she watched almost mesmerised by the hypnotic rhythm of the music. As she looked on, Louisa found herself feeling more than a little excited when she thought of taking Ellyn's place.

Her wish came true when Philippe walked Ellyn to her side bowing to her as he took his leave.
 He then looked at Louisa, "Demoiselle?" he asked, inviting her to take his hand. She placed hers in his. Slowly he led her to the centre of the room and they bowed. Once she had learned the few simple steps she began to relax, lost in a trance as she looked into Philippe's eyes. Without warning she felt his hand under her breast and the other on her back while his knee, placed under her bottom lifted her off her feet on high during a three quarter turn. He repeated this a number of times until she became more familiar with the steps and was pink cheeked.

While they danced Louisa felt an almost indiscernible change in their relationship as they gazed at one another. When the music ended Philippe bowed before leading her to sit beside Ellyn. Making his way over to a carved oak chest he filled three dishes with wine carrying them over to them before settling down in his own chair beside the fire.

Ellyn went on to name the different dances they would do on the evening of the feast. Louisa didn't recognise any of them until she heard the words, 'Scottish dances'. She laughed, "I can do those. They are from my country". She began to reel off the names of those she had recently practised for the school dance.

Ellyn and her brother didn't recognise any of them until she got to 'Schottische'. Immediately, Ellyn pulled her to her feet as Philippe called "Schottische", to the minstrels who struck up what sounded very like 'The Fiddlers Party'. While she and Ellyn danced happily around the room.

The rest of that evening was spent in laughter before Philippe ushered them both off to their rooms.

As she settled down for the night she heard a soft knock on her door. It was Ellyn, "Are you too tired to talk ?"
"I don't think I'll be able to sleep after tonight's excitement", Louisa laughed, "most enjoyable night I've

had for a long time". The girls settled to discuss what they would wear to the feast.

Ellyn told her a little about the man she might marry. He was a widower having lost his wife and child during childbirth. He would not be marrying her for her fortune as he had his own but he needed a wife and heir. She had known him since she was a child, she liked him and believed he was fond of her. If she consented she thought it was possible in time that love would grow.

An arrangement had been made for them to meet the day before the feast. Depending on how things went Philippe could be announcing the betrothal on that night.

Unexpectedly she asked, "Do you like my brother Louisa?"

"Of course, I do", taken aback, Louisa blushed, "Why do you ask?"

"I just wondered. Do you know, that's the first time I've known him to laugh and really enjoy himself for such a long time. I believe he likes you".

"I like him too, he has been very kind to me".

"Yes, he is a kind man. He is so busy doing his duty running the estate, serving the king and protecting me but he needs someone to, care for, someone to come home to".

"I'm sure he has plenty of ladies to choose from".

"Yes, there are many but…" Ellyn trailed off.

CHAPTER 7

The rest of the week was spent in preparation for the
special night. Louisa and Ellyn were fitted for ball gowns
and involved in arrangements for decorating the grand
hall.

On the day Philippe's friend was to meet with Ellyn it
was arranged that her old nannie would act as chaperone
while Philippe invited Louisa to join him while he
inspected his land.
As the day when she was accompany him moved closer,
Louisa could not eat or sleep. She had the strangest
feeling that somehow this was the day her life would
change forever.
When it finally arrived, she felt strangely calm, as if
dissociated from the world.
Dressed in a warm gown, she joined Philippe in front of
the house just after dawn.
A pale sun sketched a long pencil of light across the hills
lying to the east as they set out. They spent the morning
travelling around farms and property on the estate before

continuing along the track leading to where the river wound through the valley.

The day warmed up as they rode through the sun-dappled woodland, the scent of wild nicotiana filling the air. Eventually Philippe pointed out a suitable place to stop and eat.

Dismounting, Philippe strode over to Louisa and putting his hands around her waist lifted her down to rest on the soft turf. After placing a skin on the surface long flat rock, he carried over the basket containing some cheese, fruit, bread and ale.

They ate and chatted, comfortable in one another's company. Philippe pointed out a church a short distance away on the other side of the woods, describing it as very beautiful. He told her he would like to show it to her and was pleased when Louisa said she would like to see it. Tidying everything away, they left the horses contentedly chomping their oats and set out walking through the long grass.

The day was still, not a sound was to be heard as they made their way along. Philippe caught Louisa's hand when she stumbled over a root sticking from the ground and the moment their hands touched she felt a tingle like a small electrical charge making its way from his hand to hers. They stood for a moment, each looking into the others eyes then Philippe placed his hand under Louisa's elbow and they continued towards the little building nestling amongst the trees.

Louisa gasped when she walked through the door. A myriad of rainbow lights where the rays of the sun touched the stained glass mullioned windows set high in the walls flickered and danced in the air.

Louisa made the sign of the cross, genuflected and slipped into one of the pews kneeling to say a short prayer aware of Philippe kneeling close beside her. The rest of the time was spent looking at the stained glass windows and his family's memorial inscriptions carved into stone slabs and brasses.

Before they left they sat once more to say a short prayer, each aware of the other. "Shall we go?" Philippe asked. Louisa nodded her head in agreement. Placing her hand on the back of the seat in front as she prepared to get to her feet, one of Philippe's hands moved to gently cover it and the same frisson, she had felt earlier sparked between them.

Philippe moved to stand on the aisle and held out a hand to her. Accepting it she stepped towards him and together they walked out into the sunlight.

He turned to look at her.

"Louisa", he whispered as she looked up into his eyes.

She couldn't speak, caught in a moment in time as he tenderly kissed her.

"I love you. Dare I hope my love is returned?"

At that moment she gave up all thought of finding her way home. Philippe was home.

"Yes", she whispered, it was all that was needed.

Philippe kissed the top of her head then she felt him put his arm around her waist and suddenly she was swept on high, over and around the trees before gliding gently back to their starting place.

Held in his arms, she was lost in a dream as they stood in the sunlit day before the church door. Philippe smiled into her eyes.

"I love you, I loved you before we met and I will love you always, no matter what happens.

I don't expect you to give me your answer just now but when I return from the war, I will ask you to do me the honour of agreeing to become my wife".

Philippe lifting both her hands to his lips kissed them.

As they walked quietly back to their horses, each contented in the other's company, Louisa gave an unexplained shiver.

For an instance she thought she heard a mocking snigger but Philippe didn't appear to have heard anything out of the ordinary.

When they reached the mansion house early in the evening Ellyn was waiting to greet them. As soon as she looked at her brother's face she smiled. Kissing Louisa then Philippe on both cheeks, she led them both into the garden when a meal for four had been laid amongst the last of the summer roses.

Once they were seated she announced shyly, "It appears that we all have something to say, shall I tell you my news first?"

Both nodded.

"Henry asked me to become his wife this afternoon. I have agreed to marry him.

Philippe clearly delighted by her news, lifted her to her feet kissing her on the top of her head.

"Now, where is the man?" he called making his way towards the hall door.

He is waiting in the library".

Henry appeared wearing a pleased grin when he heard Philippe calling his name.

Philippe slapped him on the back and heartily shook him by the hand.

Louisa realised she had seen Henry before, he was one of Philippe's business partners, a regular visitor to the house, always very courteous and softly spoken. Louisa had noticed too that his eyes always rested on Ellyn and it had occurred to her then he was more than fond of her. Her concern about Ellyn being trapped in a loveless marriage because of custom disappeared, especially when she saw her friend's shining eyes.

It was arranged that their marriage was to be celebrated in forty days when Philippe returned from serving the king.

"And what of you my two dearest loves?" Ellyn asked of Philippe and Louisa.

Before Philippe gave an answer he raised an eyebrow in Louisa's direction. She smiled her assent.

" It is my hope that two weddings will be celebrated when I return", he said smiling at Louisa.

There were cries of delight from Ellyn. Philippe called for champagne and for the rest of that evening they toasted each other happily discussing their plans for the future.

When the day of the feast arrived at last, Ellyn and Louisa spent time preparing for the celebrations. Ellyn, looking beautiful in a blue velvet gown supervised Louisa's dressing, giving her maid careful instruction particularly regarding her dark hair.

As Louisa looked at the reflection of the young woman in the moss green wild silk gazing back at her from the mirror. She barely recognised herself. How much time had passed since she first arrived? Much more than she had realised. She had been so happy and contented as each day, week, month blended one into the other.

Louisa gave a little start as she heard Ellyn's voice. "Let us go my dear sister", Ellyn spoke softly taking her by the hand and together they made their way to the top of the stairs.

The hall that was filled with chattering, laughing guests fell silent as eyes were directed towards the young women making their way down the magnificent curving staircase.

Philippe who had been standing amongst a group of giggling, wings a-quivering females extricated himself politely. Smiling broadly, he accompanied Lord Henry to stand at the bottom of the stair waiting to greet them. There were more than a few sharp intakes of breath when Philippe took Louisa's hand kissing it before placing it on his arm. Followed by Ellyn and Henry they led the guests towards the bedecked tables in the magnificent dining room.

Louisa sitting alongside Philippe, Ellyn, Henry and the other important guests at the high table was aware of the whispers and questioning stares from many of the other guests.

To Louisa's great relief medieval eating customs at a feast in no way resembled the raucous ill-mannered behaviour portrayed in the Hollywood films she had seen. The guests in fact were very mindful of etiquette and very considerate of one another.

At the end of the meal Philippe stood and the guests fell silent as he announced Ellyn's betrothal to Lord Henry amidst much toasting and celebration.

For a moment, as she listened to Philippe speaking, Louisa felt a shiver run up her spine as the familiar impression of someone watching her returned.

She tried to dismiss it. It's only natural the guests will be curious about me she told herself, but they will soon lose interest as they enjoy the meal.

However, she was unable to persuade herself. This was different.

As she cast her eyes over the room her attention had been drawn by a movement at a dark spot near one of the doors. She thought she could make out a furtive, shadowy figure standing close to one of the long tapestries that hung from on high. When she directed her gaze towards the shape, the owner obviously did not wish to be seen as it hurriedly hid behind the curtain. After the meal when the ladies were retiring to the drawing room Louisa walked close to the hanging and as they passed pretended to have lost her balance and to steady herself caught on to it pulling it aside.

There was no one there.

Louisa was glad that Ellyn was with her. Although many of the ladies smiled politely when they gave Ellyn their best wishes on her betrothal and she introduced them to Louisa, she was aware of innumerable suspicious looks from others.

Eventually the minstrels struck up. Ellyn and Louisa made their way back to the hall that had been prepared for the evening's dancing.

Extricating himself from the fluttering throng who again swarmed around him, Philippe walked towards Louisa smiling as he held out his hands to take hers in his. Together he and Lord Henry walked their ladies to the centre of the floor.

The dance music reminded Louisa of the slow and graceful Strathspey and much to her surprise she found herself dancing as if she had known the steps all her life. "You look so beautiful my angel", he whispered. "I thought I would never know happiness until I found you. The moment we met I knew we were destined to be with one another, you were the one I had been waiting for".

"Dearest Philippe", she smiled up into his eyes, "I love you too", and as she said the words she felt a strange elated joy tinged by an unexplainable sadness.

"I know I said I would wait until I returned for your answer but I can't. You will marry me?" he asked.

"Oh yes", she replied.

Without warning and to looks of amazement and gasps from the guests who stood close by he laughed aloud, lifting her off her feet swinging her around.

Ellyn and Lord Henry, watching them, their faces alight with pleasure hurried to their side. Ellyn kissing them both on each cheek as Henry clapped his friend on the back.

"Dearest, dearest sister, I am so happy", Ellyn said.

They watched Philippe speak quietly into his friend's ear and Henry smile in agreement.

Philippe looked towards the minstrels waiting patiently and called "La Volta".

Surprise crossed the faces of the guests, One or two women gasped putting their hands to their faces apparently shocked at the thought of taking part in such a provocative dance, although the look was belied by the light in their eyes.

Philippe and Lord Henry led their ladies into the middle of the floor and the dance began. Only one or two couples joined them at first but soon the joy of the dance drew many others soon filling the night with music and laughter.

The dancing continued into the early hours of the morning and after the last guests had breakfasted and began their journey home Philippe and Louisa wandered in the garden watching the sun rise in the east.

"My dear", he said, "You have made me so happy. I leave to join the king tonight and I know you would not wish me to speak of this but I must".

Louisa feeling her heart sink placed her hands over her ears.

"I must" he repeated. Listen to me", he gently pulled her hands away." If I do not return I want you to find your way back home and to safety. I dream of many happy years of marriage together but nothing in this world is certain and I would leave with an easier heart if I knew every step has been covered to keep you safe".

He continued to say he knew that Ellyn and Lord Henry would do everything in their power to protect her but if it happened that was taken out of their hands she should use the tunnels running under the house.

"Never forget my dearest," he held her close, "love is an unbreakable bond. Wherever you are I will find you no matter how long it takes or how far you travel".
Louisa stood weeping. "Come my love, dry your tears, I had to say this. Promise me you will do as I ask and I can join my king with an easy heart".
Louisa dried her tears. She would save the rest until after Philippe left, "Of course I promise. I know what you say is true", and she smiled.
Joined by Ellyn and Lord Henry they attended morning Mass before returning to the hall to their morning meal. The rest of that day was spent with Ellyn and Henry as they accompanied Philippe around his estate examining the defences as Ellyn went over tactics with the womenfolk and those left behind who would be fit enough to mount a defence against an enemy.

When the time came for him to leave he drew Louisa into the garden. Kissing her, he producing a little bag

from inside his cloak removed two golden bands
engraved with two interlinked hearts.

" I had these especially made my dearest love", he said
taking her hand in his. "Wear this for me", he smiled,
slipping the smallest one onto her finger kissing it. "I
will place it on your finger once more on the day we
marry".

Louisa, afraid to speak because of the lump in her throat,
kissed his hand, "I will", she whispered raggedly as she
in turn placed the larger one on his finger.

They embraced then dry eyed Louisa let him go.

After kissing Ellyn on the cheek and shaking Henry by
the hand he mounted his horse. Lifting an arm in
farewell to the gathered company he flicked the reins and
his mount moved off.

As Louisa with a sinking heart stood for a while listening
to the sound of his horse's hoofs disappearing into the
distance, a clear memory of her holding her weeping
mother's hand while she said goodbye to her father who

stood in uniform with a kitbag by his side flashed before her mind's eye.

"My Dad came home, so will Philippe", she comforted herself.

Excusing herself she went back to the garden and as her mother had, she wept.

CHAPTER 8

The days melted one into the other. Louisa trying not to think, went about her duties as always with Ellyn. In the evenings she sat wrapped up warm in the garden hoping for the sound of Philippe's steed approaching in the distance. News of the war was slow in reaching them. What little there was told that things were not going well for the Fae army.

One afternoon as she sat in the garden, she heard the sound of a horse's hooves grow closer. Philippe! she thought, allowing herself to raise her hopes.
However, disappointment dashed them into the dust. It wasn't Philippe. An exhausted, blood stained messenger appeared out of the trees bearing news of a massive defeat.
He reported that the heavily outnumbered Fae army had been crushed during a battle.
The advancing soldiers were obliterated by enemy artillery, thousands were killed and wounded.
There was no news of Philippe who had last been seen in the thick of the fray.

Ellyn instructed that the messenger was fed and his horse watered while they sat extracting every morsel of news. After he was rested he mounted once more, taking the awful news to the other great houses.

When he left a pale-faced, Ellyn took charge. She had been expecting this but had not want to worry Louisa unduly. News had filtered through earlier about a murderous Outlander attack on a village on the south coast. Almost every man, woman and child had been slain in what the Outlanders claimed was retribution for past deeds by their enemy. Now they were pressing further north.

Now as they prepared for the enemy attack one closer to home threatened, launched by their own countrymen against the supporters of the king.

As they tightened their defences, Louisa was relieved to see reinforcements arriving when Lord Henry with a company of men rode through the gates.

As darkness approached Louisa became more and more apprehensive in the uncanny silence as they watched from the turrets. There was no movement or sound. While she waited she allowed her thoughts to stray for a moment to Philipp. She felt for the comfort of his ring that she had threaded on to a thin ribbon and placed around her neck.

Suddenly a rushing sound filled the air as hundreds of heavy stones hurled by a massive trebuchet about two hundred yards away rained down on them. Opposite and closer, missiles were launched from the bucket shape at the end of the long arm of the mangonel causing further heavy damage, serious injury and death. Then Louisa was aware of the sound of breaking glass as a hail of flaming arrows flew through the air. Suddenly fear left her as she braced herself standing with her crossbow in her hands and halberd by her side.

She fought long and hard repelling the advancing soldiers for a considerable time until she was struck on the head by one of the stones from the trebuchet. Dazed and with blood streaming into her eyes she fell against the wall. Staggered towards the turret stair she wiped the blood from her face as her vision left her while she slowly began to descend. Blackness began to engulf her when she moved her head but strive as she might to retain consciousness it eluded her.

It was the malodorous stench of sweat and urine that awakened her. Opening her eyes she was aware of lying propped up against the cold wall at the bottom of the turret steps. A red eyed, toothless grimy face covered in grey hair was leaning over her. Sinking to its knees it shuffled closer its stinking breath almost overwhelming her as it glared into her eyes. She shrunk back. Was it a man? Surely not.

Giving a laugh of triumph it shoved a stinking, black-nailed hand forward, ripping her blouse as it thrust it inside to catch hold of the ring hanging around her neck. Suddenly there was an almighty howl as a black shape, back arched, bristles erect, launched itself at him bringing him down as it sunk its teeth into his neck. He fell back under the weight.

It was Siddi who then sat back on his haunches beside Louisa, growling warnings. Clasping his neck, uttering curses the thing crawled off.

"I've got to get back to the fight, Siddi". Louisa regained her feet but head swimming she could not let go of the stone wall.

Siddi running towards a curtain in the far wall, kept stopping and looking back at her, making a series of soft growls and whispering sounds as if encouraging her to follow. Making a last effort to return to the battle she stopped.

Her eyes were surely playing tricks. It couldn't be but it was. A short distance away, Philippe with his hand stretched out to her stood smiling, looking just as he had the day they parted, "Louisa", he called, "This way. Hurry my love". He held a curtain aside for her.

"Philippe", she cried, moving towards him. "is it you? Are you all right? I thought I had lost you",

Like the sighing wind she heard him whisper,

"Remember, I will always love you".

Before she knew it, she was through the curtained doorway.

Looked back to Philippe she could see no sign of him. Siddi gave her a little nudge to move on as the door opened once more, "Philippe!" she cried, but it was Ellyn and a number of children pushing their way through.

"Did you see Philippe?" she cried to Ellyn who looked concernedly at her, "He was standing by the curtain a moment ago. You must have seen him".

Ellyn gave a stifled sob.

"Louisa, it wasn't Philippe. Hurry!"

"Of course it was, you must have seen him", she insisted refusing to move.

"Oh, my dear it could not have been Philippe", she paused for a moment, "I am so sorry to tell you at a time like this, but I have just heard the terrible news that my brother fell in battle. Our hearts are broken but there is no time for tears at the moment. You must come now, it's what Philippe would want. Quickly! Henry is waiting for us, we will be safe with him".

"No! Oh no!" Louisa cried. You are mistaken, Ellyn. I have just spoken to Philippe".

All at once the door opened once more and she was caught up in another rush of people fleeing for their lives, carrying her along with them and separating her from Ellyn.

Calling out to one another's name their voices faded as the distance between them grew.

Entangled in the headlong tumult of panicking people Louisa was propelled along dark passageways.

Stretching out a hand hoping to find something that would that help slow her down, she felt a narrow recess in the in the rock. Catching onto a piece of rock jutting close by she grasped it tightly and threw herself into the niche. Attempting to recover her breath she stood trying to think of how she could find her way back to Ellyn.

The crowd fled by and suddenly all was silent. Louisa stood listening for Philippe. He'll find me she thought. But time passed and there was no sign of him.

He couldn't be dead, Ellyn is mistaken… she has to be…she began to weep.

Peering into the darkness she heard a soft growl and saw Siddi.

"Dear Siddi", she wept, "my Philippe is gone!"

Siddi gave a tiny 'mew' nudging her towards a greyish opening along the passageway. Forcing herself not to think she allowed herself to be manoeuvred through the entrance. It was one of the tunnels Ellyn had spoken of. As they made their way along, she heard the sound of heavy, dragging footsteps accompanied by a familiar unpleasant fetid smell moving closer.

Her eyes fixed on the pale glow in the distance, she quickened her footsteps towards it.

After a few minutes she gave a soft cry of relief when she came upon two coracles each with its own paddle and tied to iron rings in the rocky wall. A little further on she saw an expanse of water, too wide and probably too deep to wade across. Beyond that she could just make out what looked like a landing stage on the far side.

"Looks like we have no choice Siddi", she said to her companion, "we will have to row across".

Hurriedly untying one of the little boats, she grabbed both paddles and throwing them into it dragged it to the water's edge.

Stepping into the river she began to push the vessel out until the water reached well past her knees then she pulled herself into it, her heart pounding as she listened to the snarling curses of her pursuer.

"Come on Siddi", she urged, "Jump!"

Siddi's black body flew gracefully through the air to land weightlessly at Louisa's feet before settling down while she paddled like mad praying there were no leaks.

Once a few yards out on the river she looked back over her shoulder to see a dark, cloaked shape at the water's edge. She heard roaring oaths as it jumped in, arms outstretched, determined to catch hold of their boat. Louisa grabbing the paddle in both hands, all fear dissipated, was determined to go down fighting. However, she could hardly believe her luck when all at once, just as the terrifying figure was in reach of the boat he stopped. Enraged as he felt his feet sucked into the coagulating mud of the bottom of the river, he grabbed handfuls of mud from he river bank throwing them furiously at her, That didn't last because in no time at all he was up to his neck in water with a look of amazed disbelief in his black eyes before disappearing beneath the surface.

Relief swept over Louisa as she returned her attention paddling and soon grasped the idea of how to set the boat in a straight course across the river towards their destination.

As they grew closer to the landing stage, she peered carefully at a brightly painted sign displaying the figures of a woman and a black cat below which the words, 'Traveller's Landing' were printed.

CHAPTER 9

When they were close enough Siddi leapt on to the wooden boards. Following him, Louisa secured the craft to a bollard. Looking back across the river to check if anyone was following, she was relieved to see only a few swans and ducks amongst the reeds.

Three paths led away from the landing.
"Which one shall we take Siddi, left or right or the one straight ahead?" she pondered.

"Oh youm makes up yourn own mind my dear. No goodn askin yon cat".

Louisa gave a start. Standing close to Siddi was a little man no more than three feet tall, wearing a brown tunic and leggings, his shaggy brown hair straggling out from under a pointed cap. He held out a web-fingered hand to her.
"Name o' Yarn, Marrofat Yarn. How d' do me dearie".
Clasping his proffered hand which reminded her of fine sandpaper, she felt hers shaken vigorously.

"I am well enough thank you sir, just a little tired and looking a bed and for work. My name is…", it was on the tip of her tongue, "it is…", but she could not for the life of her remember what her name was.

His twinkling, starry eyes on each side of a button nose looked seriously into hers.

"Bettern youm gets out o' here soon. Yon boggart do more'n throw mud at youm if he catches youm. Your'n can do wors'n than follow'n Mr Marrofat Yarn to yon farm".

Politely he doffed his hat and bowed before taking his leave of her.

Bemused, Louisa watched him make his way along the stony track whistling cheerily.

"What do you think, Siddi, he seems to know where he is going. Shall we follow him? If it doesn't work we can turn back and try the other paths".

The words were no sooner said than Siddi, with a purr bounded ahead following the little man until they both disappeared into the morning mist. Louisa picking up her bundle followed behind.

The sun shone brightly, soon drying her mud spattered clothes as she made her way along. For the first mile she kept turning around to make sure no one was following and was reassured to see the road was empty.

When she began see some shapes in the distance which could well be a few cottages, she felt the tight knot of tension in her middle begin to dissolve.

She was tired, thirsty and hungry and hopefully she could find the farm Mr Yarn had spoken of and perhaps some work.

The fields on each side were dotted with small, golden flanked cows contentedly chewing the cud and lowing contentedly as their large, white-ringed dark eyes watched her pass.

Not much further on she reached the village green drawn there by the aroma of a large hog being roasted on a spit. Louisa, exhausted by this time sat on a stone bench beside two pails of creamy milk savouring the tantalizing smell.

No sooner had she sat down when an old woman, a young man in her wake, bustled across the grass towards her,

"Lucy May! Lucy May! Where have you been? And look at that milk lying in the sun, it will go off in no time. And your dress! How did you get your dress in that state, it's filthy. Oh and it stinks", she wafted the air with a plump hand then grasped Louisa by the arm pulling her to her feet. Louisa, who had been looking around for a Lucy May, was speechless.

"Come along, come along, let's get you cleaned".

The slim, tall, young man with tousled brown hair giving her a sympathetic smile lifted the two pails of milk.

"Take them to the house, Phil", the old woman ordered.

"Right Mrs Mellon", he gave a cheery smile and lifting one in each hand began walking down the road.

Louisa who still could not find her voice, allowed herself to be propelled in the direction of a farmyard where a large metal pump stood over a wide trough.

"Leave your clothes there", The woman pointed to what looked like a kitchen door, "I'll leave you a clean dress and pinafore in your room. Don't be long now, and do give your hair a good wash and brush".

Thrusting a bar of rough looking soap and a towel into Louisa's hand she gave a "Hurrumph!" and left her.

Louisa stripped off her dirty clothes, they certainly were smelly and she was glad to be rid of them.

The water was icy cold and although it was a bit of a shock and she shivered, it certainly was a relief to be clean. She found a little gold ring attached to a piece of ribbon hanging around her neck. Examining it she saw it was engraved with two hearts. For a moment she almost grasped a memory, then it was gone and an unexplainable sadness almost overwhelmed her.

The heat from the sun soon dried her hair as she brushed it, wondering what was going to happen next.

The old woman appeared to think her name was Lucy May. The next time she saw her she would tell her she was mistaken, her name was not Lucy May.

"My name is not Lucy May", she'd say, "it is… my name is…", it was just on the tip of her tongue but try as she might, just as it was when she spoke to Mr Yarn, she just could not bring it to mind.

Dumping her soiled clothes at the kitchen door and stepping inside she made her way to a little bedroom apparently familiar with the layout of the house, which surprised her when she thought about it later.

After donning the clean underwear that had been left on the bed, she pulled on a pale blue dress that reached almost to her ankles. Next she lifted the white pinafore placing it over the dress and tying the tapes behind her. Standing in front of the mirror brushing her dark hair she was rather surprised to see the serious grey-eyed girl looking back at her. Instinctively she patted the ring lying against her heart once again that familiar sense of loss and sadness she had experienced a few minutes earlier enveloped her. However, try as she might to focus her mind on a cause for this, it continued to evade her.

"Lucy May!" once again the querulous voice of the old woman reached her, "Hurry up! You have no time to stand around dreaming as usual. I need you to help Phil carry some things to the village green. He can't do all your work for you."

Louisa hurried to the kitchen where four baskets of warm, freshly-baked bread stood on the dresser. Phil was in the process of lifting two of them as she arrived. He smiled shyly at her as she in turn lifted hers.

"And don't be late back tonight, the door will be locked at midnight!"

As they made their way to the Green, Phil said, "Don't mind Ma Melon, it's just her way. You'll soon get used to her once you've been here awhile.".

I don't think so, Louisa thought to herself.

They delivered the bread to one of the large marquees standing on the green.

"Are you hungry?" Phil asked. " Now we have delivered the bread we are free to enjoy the rest of the day. I don't suppose you know many people here so I wondered if you would like to have a picnic with me. I wrapped some food for us and put it in my pack. We could sit and eat it over there under that tree on the far side". He pointed towards a seat nestling under a tree.

"Thank you, that would nice", Louisa agreed, only now realising how hungry she was.

Together they wandered over to the tree in the dappled shade.

"Make yourself comfortable", Phil told her as he spread out a clean white cloth between them on the seat and proceeded to place pieces of creamy cheese, two rosy-cheeked apples, the still warm loaf and milk in the centre. Watching him set out the food Louisa experienced a distinct feeling of déjà vu but as before the reason for this was beyond her.

As they ate, once or twice Louisa looked up to catch Phil looking at her. Embarrassed he looked away but not before she saw the puzzled expression he wore.

They sat enjoying the peace while watching the preparations for the festival as the aroma of the pig roast wafted in their direction.

"Do you live close by, Phil?" Louisa asked. "Are you a farmer?"

"No, I'm only staying for another three weeks until I go to university to study law. My family are close friends of the owner and when I was offered the opportunity to make some money I jumped at it. What about you, will you stay?"

"Oh no. I have been travelling and must make my way home soon", without thinking, the words tripped naturally from Louisa's tongue.

Contented they sat quietly together enjoying the warmth of the day.

Phil cleared his throat a few times as if preparing to ask her something. Louisa waited but nothing happened. Just as she thought that he had probably changed his mind he blurted, "Do you already have arrangements made with someone to accompany you to the celebration? If not would you like to come with me?" He sat there looking embarrassed. "Sorry, that isn't how I meant it to sound". Louisa smiled, "I know what you mean and yes, I would like to go with you".

While they sat watching the dignitaries beginning to take their places on the raised platform that acted a stage, Phil scattered what was left of the loaf and the two apple cores for the birds before slinging his knapsack over his shoulder. He proffered a hand to Louisa who, after removing her pinafore and smoothing down her dress, accepted it.

The speeches had already started when they reached the stage. They were just in time to hear the mayor introducing the guests of honour, Lord Henry of Elveshome, a handsome man with a military bearing and his wife Lady Ellena, a beautifully elegant looking woman in pale lilac.

"Where on earth have you been Phil?" The childish voice of pretty dark haired young girl of around thirteen, wearing a pink muslin dress tugged at Phil's arm. "Pa and Ma wondered where you had disappeared to. Oh hello," she caught sight of Louisa, "who are you? My name is Louisa Rose". Louisa just had time to acknowledge her when she shouted, "There's Marigold, everyone keeps vanishing today", and she darted off towards the figure of another young girl in a gauzy bright yellow dress shouting, "Marigold , where have you been? Do wait for me! Have you found Violet or Petunia yet?" Catching up with Marigold they clasped hands and together they flitting off to look amongst the flowers for their friends.

Just like pretty butterflies, Louisa thought to herself.

"That's my youngest sister", Phil explained, "she never stays long in the same spot to hold a conversation".

They stood for a moment or two until Lord Henry had finished speaking.

"Would you like to meet my parents?" he said. Louisa who had been looking around the guests trying to guess who they might be, felt his hand on her elbow as he guiding her towards the smiling guests of honour who had just made their way from the stage.

"Pa, Ma", he said when they reached them, "I'd like you to meet my friend Louisa. Louisa, this is my mother Lady Ellena and my father Lord Henry". Louisa had the oddest, happy, sad feeling that she had met them before but she couldn't have, could she wondered. Curtseying to cover her confusion, she smiled politely.

" It is very pleasant to meet you, my dear", Phil's mother kissed her on the cheek .

Phil's father, giving her a slightly surprised look inclined his head. " A pleasure, young lady".

Louisa smiled in return.

After spending a few moments in conversation Phil took leave of his parents who then wandered off to mingle with the rest of the guests.

Louisa, still aware of an odd sense of loss felt herself relax a little as they threw balls at the coconut shy, hoops around little yellow ducks floating in the pond, ate candy floss and enjoyed all the fun of the fair.

When evening arrived and the sky grew darker coloured lanterns strung amongst the trees illuminating the village green in a gentle glow. Phil made sure that Louisa was comfortable on a blanket on the grass while she waited for him to collect a plate of hot sizzling pork with tomatoes and lettuce. As he made his way back to her and she watched him balance both plates of food, she caught her breath sharply. There it was again. That elusive memory filled with a strange mix of sadness and joy. For a moment, as he approached, he stopped as if perplexed trying to remember something too as another puzzled look crossed his handsome young face. Then, appearing to dismiss his thoughts he continued towards her.

The pork in slices between two thick slices of fresh bread was filled with flavour. When she finished and had wiped her fingers on her pinafore, she sat elbows on knees , chin resting on her hands, watching the reflection of the full moon on the duck pond.

Suddenly there was bang and a voice, followed by those of others shouted, "Boggart!"

Louisa looking in the directing the noise was coming from was taken aback to see a cow on the other side of the pond racing in her direction. A crowd were following shouting instructions to one another about the best way to capture it.

They're scaring the poor thing it's going to end up in the pond. I hope it isn't too deep, she thought as she watched the frightened animal.

As it got closer, all at once she realised she was in its line of flight and in danger but she couldn't move. Without warning she felt herself pushed out of the way as the cow, rather than running into the water launched itself to sail over the moon's reflection landing where Louisa had been sitting a moment ago.

One of Phil's friends caught hold of the rope hanging around its neck causing it to swing around and stop.

"Come on girl, easy, easy now", He spoke softly into the terrified animal's ear.

"This's been done deliberately", he said, examining the rope tethered around the animal's neck. Look, that's a clean cut".

He bent down to examine the beasts hoofs, "Looks like scorch marks. Only a boggart would do that", he shook his head in disgust. "Could have killed yon lass", he nodded in Louisa's direction.".

Phil put his arm around Louisa's shoulders thinking to comfort her but for some reason she felt nothing. Everything felt so unreal as if it was happening to someone else.

Eventually, after the cow was returned to the byre and everyone settled down, a tall, slack-haired young man with a fiddle struck up a lively jig and everyone joined in the dancing.

Phil's friends sat with them and as they laughed and joked Louisa allowed her attention to wander.

All at once her eyes were drawn towards what could have been a figure moving amongst the dark area of trees and bushes on the out-skirts of the field. She shivered wondering if her pursuer made it to the landing after all but all she could make out were the shadows of branches caught in the gentle breeze. Almost, but not entirely successfully dismissing it from her mind, she brought her attention back to the cheerful company.

Later, Phil walked her safely back to the farm and saw her inside the kitchen door. She was taken aback when she saw the sink filled with dirty dishes and the floor covered in muddy footsteps.

"I supposed I had better set to and get this lot cleared up before I go to bed. And what's this?" Puzzled she looked at a jug of thick cream, a plate of tiny cakes, some corn muffins and a dish of golden honey set out on a low bench.

She walked towards the sink when Phil caught her by the arm. "Just leave everything as it is Louisa. Mr Yarn likes to sort this out", he waved his hand over the dirty dishes and muddy floor. "And these", pointing towards the cakes and milk on the bench, "are treats for Mr Yarn. Not payments for his work mind you, never payments, merely treats".

 Phil sounded as if his words were meant not only for Louisa's ears but she couldn't see anyone else in the kitchen.

Suddenly overwhelmed by tiredness she agreed to do as Phil asked, wished him goodnight and went into her room.

Still rather unnerved by the incident with the cow and the shadows in the trees, she placed a chair back under the handle of the bedroom door and making sure the windows were secure.

Eventually she fell into an uneasy sleep disturbed by dreams of being chased by a dark figure dressed in a black cloak with a hood pulled over his head.

Awakened by the cock crowing at dawn she arose, washed and dress then made her way through the kitchen in the semi darkness. To her surprise it was sparkling clean, the dishes displayed on the dresser shelves. The floor scrubbed and polished.

She walked to the byre intending to help milk the cows but apparently Mr Yarn had already been there before her, fresh milk in churns, cows in the meadow, byre scrubbed and cleaned. Turning back to the kitchen she saw a place had been set for her where a plate of porridge with a jug of creamy, warm milk was set in her place.

After she had finished she collected two pails of milk and made her way towards town with them.

Two weeks later as the birds were beginning their dawn chorus and the weak sun lent a pale glow from the east, as usual, Louisa carried her burdens along the track towards town. She shivered, noticing that the weather was not as warm as it has been when she felt a nip of frost in the air. Time I was moving on she thought regretfully, perhaps wait another two weeks, then I really must go.

The following week the weather became much colder and one morning she awoke to find a few flakes of snow lying on the grass. Although they soon melted, Louisa felt the difference in the air as she went about her work that day.

Returning in the evening, after supper she went to her room and began to pack her bag, leaving out what few warm clothes she owned.

She listened to Mr Yarn humming to himself as he shuffled about cleaning the kitchen. Shivering in the cold she undressed then cuddled down in bed and dozed off.

Awakened suddenly from a deep sleep she sat up. Something was different.

Opening her eyes, she found her room was bathed in a pearly glow. Swinging her legs out of bed she wrapped her shawl around her shoulders and making her way to the window she moved the curtains aside.

Unable to see anything through the freezing window she breathed on it in an attempt to clear away the ice crystal patterns that were beginning to form. A patch in the glass cleared enough to allow her to see a magnificent, sparkling star lighting the sky. The air was white, filled with snowflakes descending in gauzy veils. Gazing intently through the cleared space for a few minutes, all at once she realised what she was looking at were not flakes of snow but miniscule winged creatures dressed in silvered white, whirling and fluttering in their hundreds upon hundreds from the sky down a path of incandescent light leading from the star to the grass. Some settled to carpet it in a thin layer of sparkling whiteness while others huddling together in large groups drifted against the bottom of the hedge.

Startled by a mellifluous voice close to her ear she jumped.
"Time to leave for home, my dear. Many more of my friends will join us before the night is over and by then it will be too late". The voice was sweet and clear.
Louisa's eyes were drawn to an iridescent creature hovering above the nightstand. Its head appeared to rotate yet its eyes never left her face.
It's a white own, a magical white owl, she thought.
"Who are you? Why are you here?" she asked.
"I have been appointed to see you safely on your way", the light flickered.

"Wear this", it said pointing to a white downy coat of feathers lying at the bottom of the bed, "it will keep you warm. Once you begin your journey do not, no matter how tired you are" she repeated, "do not fall asleep in the snow. There are those who prize the soul of a young mortal and would wish to keep you".

Astonished, Louisa could only stand looking at her. There were so many questions she wanted to ask but as she thanked the being, it began to melt and disappear from sight. She sat quietly on the bed for a moment wondering if she had been dreaming then looked at the coat.

She turned to the window when all at once something banged against it. Startled, she jumped back as a black head suddenly appeared and two silvery eyes gazed into hers. "Siddi!", she exclaimed with relief, her heart beating fast, "Siddi!" raising the window. "You must be frozen, quickly, come inside".

The cat gave a quiet mew.

Before closing it again she looked out hoping to see her unexpected visitor outside, but only the snow fairies lay there, cuddled together.

"Time to be going Siddi, before the snow settles in and I'm trapped here".

She heard a gentle knock on the bedroom door. Opening it carefully, she found a little knapsack lying on the carpet. Taking it into the room she opened it to see some freshly baked scones, cheese and warm rolls wrapped up neatly. "bless you Mr Yarn", she whispered.

Pulling on a warm jumper, tunic and leggings she thrust her feet into warm socks and boots. After checking to make sure the gold ring she carried on the ribbon around her neck was still there, she wrote a quick note to say goodbye to Mrs Mellon and one to Phil apologising for her hasty departure.

Pulling on the white coat and finally a knitted hat over her ears she looked out of the window. All was clear so quietly pushing it up she and Siddi climbed out into the cold night air.

The moon lit her way as she followed the cat's prints along the road towards the point where they first landed. As they walked, she had the uncomfortable feeling of being followed but noticed the snow was rapidly covering her footsteps.

"Thank you snow fairies", she whispered, "if that boggart is trying to catch me, he won't have any tracks to follow".

Siddi had reached the landing stage before her and sat patiently waiting for her.

"Which way?" she wondered, considering the choices. She'd had three choices when she first arrived and she had chosen the path to the left. "Better make my mind up soon", she shivered, tightening her cloak around herself. "The snow is getting heavier and we'll need to find shelter soon.

As she considered the best path to take her attention was caught by the board which no longer depicted 'Traveller's Landing' but a map showing three paths leading away.

Above the path to the left someone had scrawled,

'Been there, done that!'

The path leading straight ahead, 'Not such a good idea!'

While the path to the right showed a thumbs-up sign accompanying the words, 'Might be worth a try!'

"Seems like the road on the right might be best, Let's try that one, Siddi".

As she spoke the words on the board slowly disappeared to be replaced by a crudely drawn arrow pointing along the path that went straight ahead with the words,

'They went thataway!'

Smiling, Louisa and the cat set off at a brisk pace.

Walking became difficult as the snow lay thicker on the ground. Louisa fell behind Siddi and after an hour she was barely able to make out the cat's footprints.

She was so tired and was beginning to feel the time had come to find some shelter when she heard a muffled sounding shout behind her.

Turning around her heart leapt as she could just make out a crouching figure in a dark cloak in the whiteness lumping along almost upon her.

Panicking, she pushed herself forward but her foot slipped on something hard and she fell onto a low stone dyke. She heard Siddi give a soft 'mew' from the other side and finding a foothold she threw herself over it to land in the soft white snow on the other side.

Thanks to her long white coat she appearing as part of the snow-covered wall. She lay close to it, holding her breath as she listened to the heavy breathing and angry grunts from the other side as the creature moved slowly along the wall searching for her. As the sound grew fainter, she heard a soft purring sound, she looked to see Siddi covered in snow his crystal eyes gazing into hers. "Oh Siddi," she almost wept, "I don't have the energy to run any further. Go now, save yourself".

Leaning on one elbow and pushing herself into a sitting position it occurred to her that she had not been lying flat. She felt the land sloping away from her and for a moment the falling snow seemed to ease enough to allow her to make out what appeared to be a steep downward slope about a yard away, disappearing into the white distance.

She heard a soft growl from the cat as he dug close to the wall where an object stuck out a few inches above the snow.

"What is it Siddi?" Louisa saw he was sitting beside a larger object that had been partially covered by snow. On her knees she moved towards it and began to push the snow away until enough was visible for her to take hold of. She pulled at it but it hardly moved being bigger and heavier than she expected. Siddi kept digging, throwing the snow to the side.

Taking a deep breath, she used all of her strength in an effort to dislodge it. It moved only slightly at first, before all at once, it came loose flying over her head to land upside down behind her beginning to slide slowly down the incline.

She thrust out two hands grabbing it before it gathered momentum and disappeared into the whiteout.

"Oh, I don't believe it, Siddi you clever thing, it's a sledge. Let's get it upright".

As soon as she righted it she became aware of laboured breathing getting closer and a rancid stink coming from the other side of the wall. It must have heard them! Horrified she saw a thickset shape appear above the wall, growling menacingly as it began to clamber across. Barely taking time to get comfortable Louisa pushed the sledge to the top of the incline and jumped on. Clutching her bundle of belongings and knapsack between her knees, with Siddi in front of her she pushed off. The sledge took only a second before gathering speed escaping from the grip of the angry, roaring thing in the black cloak and raced into the whiteout.

Faster and faster flew the sledge as if on wings barely touching the surface. Gathering momentum, it effortlessly travelled up inclines and over the top before hurtling downwards once more.
At first Louisa felt elated by their escape but as the night darkened, she was beginning to despair of the journey ever ending. She needed to sleep but fought to keep her eyes open.

All at once, for no apparent reason the sledge began to slow down.

Moving, as if guided by an invisible hand it travelled towards the side of the track coming to rest under a canopy of leafless trees.

Relieved and hungry, Louisa made herself comfortable and opened the knapsack to take out the parcel made up by Mr Yarn. To her surprise it seemed much larger than it had at first. There was a chunk of creamy cheese, muffins and scones, warm as if just removed from the oven. A jug of warm milk which miraculously had not spilled had been tucked in a compartment at the side together with a bottle of cream and a box containing biscuits and a packet of salmon with Siddi's name clearly printed on it.

After Louisa removed a mug for herself and a saucer for Siddi, they both tucked in as Louisa offered up a silent prayer for Mr Yarn.

After they had finished, Louisa tidied everything away and relaxed on the sledge.

Unexpectedly, to her surprise she heard the laughing voices of children.

Looking in the direction from which they came she could make out a number of little white, fur-enclosed figures, some snowballing, while others pushed a large ever-growing snowball in her direction.

When they reached Louisa, they stopped to gaze intently at her. They all looking exactly the same, their black eyes shining with curiosity and little button noses wrinkling in delight as they peeped shyly from their large furry hoods.

She heard an excited whisper, "It's a mortal", accompanied with gasps of delight.

"You look tired," a piping voice observed. "Have you come far?"

"I have come a long way and yes, I am very tired".

Louisa felt weariness like a great wave wash over her.

"Then you should sleep. Sleep and stay with us", another voice urged.

"Sleep... sleep...sleep". Various whispering voices fell upon her ears like snowflakes.

"Let us remove that heavy coat and fold you in snowflakes. You will find them much softer and warmer".

Louisa felt little hands removing her coat and gently covering her with snow. "Sleep now, and stay with us". "Oh yes", she breathed sinking into a most marvellous peacefulness.

All at once, Siddi gave an ear-splitting howl, the sledge gave a shudder and began to edge slowly back towards the track.

 Shaken back to wakefulness, Louisa disoriented, found herself snuggling into Siddi's warm fur.

"Oh, don't leave us!" she heard the sound of dismayed, silvery voices fading in the distance., "We love you. Please stay...Don't go...".

The sledge moved very slowly to the crest of what looked like a very steep downward slope descending towards a narrow valley before ascending steeply again into the darkness.

Holding on tightly, Louisa waited with baited breath while it paused, as if it were alive and preparing itself for take-off. Then once more it began to move slowly, so slowly at first, then with increasing speed until it was flying at a tremendous pace, the wind tearing Louisa's hat from her head and her hair streaming stiffly behind. Down, down into the valley, they reached it in a breath before the acceleration carried them with a 'whoosh' through it before sending them hurtling upwards towards the top of the next hill.

Suddenly Louisa felt the sledge hit something hard. All at once both she and Siddi, with an indignant screech, were sent flying through the air arriving with a 'BUMP!' on something soft.

CHAPTER 10

Louisa opened her eyes. She was lying on her back, her landing cushioned by a scratchy but pliable material as she listened to a cacophony of voices shouting instructions, horns being blown loudly, sheep bleating, geese honking, costermongers offering their wares from somewhere below her.

Siddi, winded, was lying on his side.

Louisa felt decidedly sick as a swaying motion took hold of whatever they were caught up in. Raising herself up a little and looking around, she saw they had landed amongst a large pile of sacks enclosed in a tarry-smelling, heavy rope netting which had been gathered together and caught on a large hook that was swaying backwards and forwards. Pushing her face as close to the sides as she dared she could see they were suspended above a wharf swarming with shouting stevedores loading and unloading various cargoes. Holding on to the rope she pulled herself upright until she had a view through the misty morning of various other docks where ships were stationed some with passenger and luggage embarking and disembarking.

The rope net holding them aloft gave a sudden jolt as it was swung out further over the wharf and slowly began to descend. "Quickly Siddi", she urged, "hide under the sacks. Escape when you can and we'll find one another later".

Heaping the sacking over their heads, Louisa flattened herself as much as she could. She could feel herself slowly descending and once on the ground heard the rope that was securing everything being released. She watched, heart in mouth as a large tarry hand began to slowly loosen the netting and free the sacks. Louisa preparing to run the minute she was discovered, held tightly to her bag.

As she crouched waiting, blood pumping in her ears, she heard Siddi give an ear-splitting howl and felt him springing high into the air. There were shouts as shocked men fell back when the large black shape launched itself over their heads. For a few moments stunned silence reigned as they turned around to look at the creature, back arched and bristles erect staring at them before turning and speeding off. The silence was broken by relieved laughter when the men realised this was not a monster but a large cat.

One of the workers gave chase but Siddi was far too agile, successfully evading the man every time he tried to catch hold of him.

Slipping from her hiding place while the men were distracted, she heard one of them call, "Let him go, Charlie, It's probably the ship's cat. He'll soon find his way back".

Muttering about never knowing what was going to be hiding amongst the cargo they returned to unloading the sacks.

Grasping her bundle close, Louisa made her way around the water filled tanks filled with crabs, lobsters and other strange looking, coloured crustaceans of every shape and size. A teeming throng of men, women and children selling whelks and seafood of every description shouted their wares as they stood by the waterside. A little further back a thriving, bustling, market-place displayed lengths of silk, cotton, lace, embroidered tablecloths, lace doilies, children's clothing, trinkets, good luck charm and all kinds of merchandise.

Louisa stopped for a moment trying to think what her next move. She needed to find somewhere to stay the night but as she did not having any money that posed a problem.

She became aware of something pulling at her skirt and looking down saw a pretty face smiling up at her. At first she thought it belonged to a child.

"What do you want my little love", she asked. "Are you lost?'

" Oh not me my dear, it's you what's lost an' needs shelter". The voice that answered sounded much older than she had expected it would. Then surprised and somewhat embarrassed she realised she was not speaking to a child at all but a rather pretty looking little lady whose long silvery hair was threaded with what looked like long strands of seaweed.

"Oh, I am so sorry, I…".

The lady held up a hand, "A common mistake me dear. Not to worry. I been expecting you, been waiting since dawn. It was that big cat sidth what alerted me to where you might be".

The lady took Louisa's hand in hers and led her between two of the stalls to a flap at the back. Pulling it carefully to one side they stepped through.

"This way. It's not far, just outside of town, a very nice little place close to the shore. Belongs to my sister in law".

As they made their way along the shore path, Louisa listened to the lady's gentle hypnotic voice singing softly. As in a dream, she remembered waves, buckets and spades, rock pools, ice cream cones and happy childhood summer days that would never end.

All at once she came back to the present to find herself standing alone outside a whitewashed cottage.

This must be the place she thought looking at the wicker gate before her.

The latch on the gate gave an odd sounding click as she lifted it then closed it behind her. She was on the point of knocking on the door to ask if there was any work when a very tall, sad looking woman wearing an apron and carrying a basket of herbs, made her way through the garden from the side of the cottage.

"Good, you've arrived. I been waitin' for you. My name is Esme. No," she held up a hand as Louisa who at last remembered her name, was going to introduce herself.

"Anonymity. Best we calls you Daisy. Much safer. What the ear does na hear, the more the claws sheathed. Come with me an eat".

Louisa didn't know what to make of this piece of wisdom but followed Esme along the path to the back door.

The cottage was much larger inside than it looked from outside. The sun slanted through the sparkling window panes casting twinkling faerie sparkles when it touched the prisms of crystal hanging from the window rails. The worn furniture smelling of beeswax gave of a warm glow. Little vases filled with wildflowers sat on the windowsills while shells of all colours and sizes sitting on little lace doilies were scattered around the room.

"Wash yourn hands an sit down here dear Daisy", Esme pulled out a chair from the table that looked like it had been scrubbed within an inch of its life. "You must be tired an' hungry".

After Louisa dried her hands she tucked her legs under the table as Esme, sitting herself opposite served generous helpings of salmon mouse, crab claws, whiting goujons and mussels along with warm bread on to each of their plates to be washed down with lemon and honey water.

Louisa had never tasted such delicious food before. She had always loved fish but this meal was heavenly.

By the time they had finished Esme's face had lost the look of sadness.

When she saw Louisa looking at her she smiled. "I am lonely, yourn bein' here will be doin' me good" she sighed looking longingly at a beautiful blue stoned ring on her wedding finger.

"Your husband?" Louisa began to ask, have you lost him?"

"Ar 'n more ways 'n one", then fell silent, thinking.

Louisa decided not to press her, no doubt she would tell her when and if she felt like it.

"Does your sister stay here too?" she asked.

Esme shook her head, "No Daisy, Sally prefers the seashore under the stars. Her visits me but has to get back outside".

Although they had just met, Esme seemed to have taken a liking to Louisa. She told her it was not safe for her to travel any further at that moment and that she was welcome to stay. She could do a little housework keeping the guest rooms clean and changing the beds for those who visited during the warmer months until it was safe for her to set out once more.

As there were only two gentleman guests at that moment all that was needed was a little ironing and setting their tables.

After they had eaten Esme showed Louisa to her room that was situated at the eves at the front overlooking the sea and shore. "What a wonderful view", she exclaimed holding the sunshine yellow curtains aside.

" An 'specially when the moons out an' the dancers wander out o' the waves. You never knows what you sees. Now not to worry, yourn safe here with Esme". As she gently patted Louisa's arm, for a moment a ripple of familiarity, enveloped her.

When Louisa expressed a wish to begin helping in the house immediately Esme smiled.
"The morrow'n soon enough. Just you take yourself along the shore, not too far mind you, get to know yourn ways around. An if happen you sees a crab or two while wanderin'", she said almost as an afterthought, "jus' pop it in yon bucket", she directed a glance towards a galvanised pail lying beside the kitchen door.

Louisa pail in hand closed the gate behind her, crossed the path to the sand dunes and wandering through them made her way towards the shore, listening as the waves lapped against the large grey rocks above sticking out of the water.
Carefully picking her way amongst the stones and shingle towards them she steadied herself as she found a footing and climbed to sit on top. A gentle breeze ruffled her hair as she looked around the shore. It was certainly a much more colourful place than other shores she was

familiar with. Adorned by glass of all colours, its edges blunted by the sea scattered about amongst the abandoned shells, faerie fan flower and sea lavender with its purple to blue clusters of flowers waving gracefully in the gentle air, painted a beautiful moving picture.

Various seaweeds were to be seen attached to rocks, red fronds of dulse, long fronds of throngweed looking for all the world like rough greenish hair while pretty peacocks tail with its fan shaped fronds adorned some of the rock pools added to the magical beauty of the place.

All at once Louisa's eye was caught by a movement in the water close by the rock on which she sat. As she gazed a rounded grey shape appeared staring at her with kindly eyes.

"Hello", she said.

The seal looked at her for a moment and gave a short bark. Submerging then appearing once more it pulled its way forward by its flippers on one of the rocks close to her, giving a short series of barks before settling down to scrutinise her.

To her surprise it was followed by four more grey seals making their way on to the surrounding rocks to share in their companion's assessment of her. Apparently deciding Louisa's presence acceptable they all settled down to enjoy the warm sun before it sunk below the horizon.

As Louisa gazed into the blue ocean she was aware of the unearthly music she had heard while she walked alongside Sally.

As the sun disappeared and its rays transformed the western sky red and gold, each seal slipped off its rock to disappear beneath the gentle waves.

Louisa deciding it was time for her to go as well, stood up and carefully climbed back on to the shingle. The pail that had been empty when she had arrived was now almost filled with sea water and contained three crabs. She couldn't think how they had got there but assumed perhaps someone had left them while she sat day dreaming.

As she bent to lift the pail her eye caught sight of something sticking out from underneath the rock she had been sitting on. Putting out a hand to feel it she felt something soft that had been wrapped in some kind of waterproof material before being hidden from view.

She caught hold of it and began to pull gently. It moved a little but became caught on something that held it back. Deciding it could take too long to uncover completely she pushed it back thinking she would try to move it the following day and continued on her way back to the cottage.

"Welcome back dear Daisy. Did you have an enjoyable time sitting by the water?" Esme greeted Louisa. "An' fine big crabs for tea too", she smiled. "Now you gets changed the tea will be on the table awaitin' you".

While they were eating their evening meal and Louisa spoke about the seals she had met that afternoon Esme's eyes took on a faraway look as the sadness returned to her face.

In an effort to take Esme's mind off whatever it was that made her so unhappy Louisa asked about the photographs that sat on the mantlepiece.

"That's my Jimbo", she said proudly, "He's a musician in a faraway land". She pointed to a cheerful looking young man of around twenty. "An' that is my darlin'

Evangeline, she's a doctor in the city". The pretty girl in the photograph smiled happily back at them.

"An' that", she lifted the photograph of a handsome man in the uniform of a seaman at the helm of a boat, "is my Henry", she held the photograph close to her heart. "He's gone now, they're all gone but I must stay".

Suddenly changing the subject she smiled, "Goin' " to be a fine night. The moon will be out soon. A night for dancing. Now you rest well an' sleep peaceful".

Wishing Esme a goodnight and thanking her for making her feel so welcome, Louisa made her way upstairs and sat on the bed feeling tiredness washing over her in waves.

The shadow of wings flying past the window disturbed the steady glow of moonlight to jolt her from her sleep. At first unsure of where she was, she lay still for a moment watching moonbeams slanting through the casement window painting the walls and pouring a dappled flood on the floor.

The night was warm, too warm to fall asleep again so Louisa made her way over to the window, pushed up the bottom pane and leaned her arms on the sill to gaze at the moon-washed sea. The gentle sound of ethereal singing mingling with that of the lapping waves caressed her ears continuing to enwrap her in their languid embrace. All at once her attention was caught by the curious little click from the gate latch. She looked down to see Esme making her way to the shore.

Thinking it was a trick of the moonlight at first, Louisa became aware of a number of female, shadowy shapes appearing from behind the rocks, arms outstretched to embrace Esme who had slipped her shift from her shoulders.

As her eyes became accustomed to the semi darkness, Louisa saw their naked bodies sleek and glowing in the light of the moon.

Esme perching gracefully on one of the rocks took the pins from her hair allowing it to flow down across her shoulder and breast began brushing it as she sang sweetly. While the rest danced, one of her companions joined her threading strands of seaweed through her hair as she softly added her voice to that of Esme's.

Listening to the magical harmony gentle waves flowed over Louisa as she journeyed through a wonderland of corals , glowing caves, brightly coloured shoals of fish and piles of golden coins and precious stones flowing from the holds of sunken ships.

A sound drew her back to the little bedroom where she leaned on the window sill, chin in hand watching them. Turning around quickly she caught sight of an odd shadow that disappeared as soon as she saw it.

Probably a cloud passing across the moon she decided, yawning and suddenly feeling tired.

Louisa arose early the following morning to be greeted by a smiling Esme who had already laid breakfast for them on the scrubbed table.

After dusting the rooms and putting fresh water in the flower vases Louisa, with a pail over her arm walk along the shore gathering shellfish to be cooked for the supper that evening. She remembered the wrapped package she had come across under the large rock but decided to let it be until later.

During supper that evening Esme sat looking at her as if making up her mind to say something. When she realised Louisa had noticed she spoke.

"I saw you awatchin' us last night, dear Daisy", she said, "you must be puzzled so tis only right I tells thee my story".

Making their way towards two comfortable chairs by the large window they settled and Esme began to speak.

CHAPTER 11

"I was not always entirely land bound", she began, "Contented, I laughed and sang with my sisters in the sea. At night, by the light of the moon we would make our way onto the rocks of the shore where we divested our pelts to take on the full body shape of two legged human beings.

One night as I sat brushing my hair a beautiful young man appeared. He was walking along the shoreline skimming flat stones into the water. My friends, gathering their pelts moved off to hide on a different part of the shore but I waited behind watching him. He was the most handsome creature I had ever seen. I returned there each evening hoping he would be there too. Sometimes he came, others he didn't. One evening after a long absence and my heart aching, he returned. I was so overjoyed I decided to make myself known to him.

He wasn't taken aback as I thought he might be because he had been aware of me all along and was willing to give me the time I needed before I decided to speak to him.

From then on we met and talked. He was a kind, gentle man. A sailor who had lived on the headland most of his life. He told me about a little whitewashed cottage he wished to purchase. It was close to the sea and would be the perfect place from which to raise a family when he met the right lass. When he asked me to be his wife I was overjoyed. On the day of our wedding I shed my pelt and hid it amongst the sand dunes determined not to wear it again.

We spent a joyful life together and had fine a son and daughter, both grown up now.

When my Henry sailed out I was always there waiting to welcome him back into my arms. Then one day he did not come back.

I waited and wept, afraid his boat had been caught in a storm and he was adrift and lost. I could have worn my pelt and gone searching but I had been so long away I was afraid that once I returned to the water there would be no way back for me and who would look after my children. My sisters searched the seas for him without success

Many years passed and my dearest never returned. I was once tempted to reclaim my pelt but when I looked it was nowhere to be seen. We meet each night as you saw us, they return to the sea in the mornings while I return to the cottage to wait".

Then Louisa remembering the package that had been hidden under the rock told Esme about it, her eyes lit up. "I wonder if it could be mine?" she whispered almost to herself.
"Two of us might be able to dislodge it", Louisa suggested.
"Thank you dear Daisy," Esme smiled, "but if you just show me the place where it lies, that will be enough".

When Louisa asked Esme about her sister in law Sally, the little lady who had met her at the docks. She confided in her that Sally had lived on the headland and been married to a fisherman. She soon found him boring and became so dissatisfied with her life that every night she made her way to join Esme and her sisters

It was on one of these nights an incredibly handsome young selkie man appeared and began to pay court to Sally. Although warned about the selkie men who deliberately sought out dissatisfied wives, she fell in love with him and left her husband who died of a broken heart.

Sally and her lover set up home but he soon grew tired of her and eventually left her. It was then she realised how much she had hurt her husband.

Since then she spent her time making atonement by seeking out those who were in danger and taking them to safety as she had Louisa.

One morning Esme announced, "I have some guests arriving, dear Daisy. A family of five, Mam an Dad, Percy age nine, Selina age six and Tommy age two".

"Lovely, it will be rather nice to have a happy family around enjoying themselves", she said looking forward to meeting them.

"Ah now there's more to it than that unfortunately. It could be a bit of a shock for you because Mum is convinced their baby is a changeling.

Sally and I might be able to help but your opinion would
be invaluable".
More than a little surprised Louisa agreed.

The family arrived the next day. Father was a tall
handsome man with worry lines etched on his forehead
unloaded the car while his wife a pale young woman,
who could have been described as pretty but for the
downward tilt of her mouth, shrieked continuously at
their two excited, energetic children. who, after rapidly
downing their lunch, immediately ran off to explore the
sea shore.

"We live in woodland", he explained rather
apologetically, "being close to the sea is a real treat for
them. It's all they have spoken about for days".
His wife had seated herself on one of the armchairs
watching a child of around eighteen months who at on
the rug rocking to and fro.
"Hello, little boy", said Louisa, "what's your name?"
The child continued to rock back and forth not paying
her the slightest of attention. When Louisa bent a little

closer to catch his large brown eyes eye he gave an ear splitting scream. She jumped back as his mother grasped him up into her arms .

" Now stop that! Look at me when I speak to you!" she hissed through closed teeth as the child continued to howl and scream and she began to shake him.

"See, see", she cried, "that's not my Tommy. My Tommy is a happy, little lad always smiling and giving me kisses. This child does not like me, he won't look at me, can't bear me to touch him. Screams all the time", she dumped him back on the rug.

"This is not my boy!", she began to weep.

"Oh dear, when did he begin to behave like this?" Esme asked sympathetically.

"It all began weeks ago when I noticed a bird that lives in the hollow beside one of the old trees begin to make a nuisance of itself. It watched Tommy, all the time coming closer and landing on Tommy's pram so that I had to 'shew' it off. It always returned to the hollow twittering all the time, as if speaking to my little boy.

One rather cold night when we sat snuggled up beside the nursery fire listening to the rain, I heard the wind gaining in strength Then the rain began to pour.

There was scratching at the window sill that got louder. I looked out and saw tiny wizened brown faces peering in at me and beyond those little misshapen figures dancing on the grass. I shouted at them to go away but they threw all kinds of things at the window pane and shouted Tommy's name. The racket continued all night. My children were asleep and unaware of what was happening. As my husband was away on business, I took Tommy into my bed. We didn't get much sleep as he tossed and turned all night, crying and throwing the bedclothes about. Eventually he fell into a restless sleep.

That morning after the children had gone to school I was relieved to see everything seemed to have returned to normal. The sun began to shine and we sat in the garden playing 'peek a boo'. After lunch my little boy kissed me then he cuddled up on my lap while I sang to him. When he fell asleep I put him in his pram in the garden just as I always did, then I sat snoozing beside him.

That was the last I saw of my little boy.

The next time I opened my eyes, the pram was empty. I screamed, ran to check the gate but it was still locked. I searched under every bush and was just giving up hope when I saw him appear from a hollow beside one of the old trees as he came crawling towards me.

But that was not my Tommy. Someone had stolen my little boy and left this child, in his place".

Tommy's mother described the events in an odd flat voice, as if she had gone over those moments over and over in her mind trying to make sense out of what had happened.

Then she pulled back his rompers to display his skinny little legs.

"Look at those!" she cried, "Not a pick on them. He eats all the time, will not stop eating us out of house and home". She pulled back the child's lips, "Almost a full set of teeth too.

We haven't had a moments luck since he appeared. The children are afraid of him".

As she prodded him, Louisa thought, to herself, Poor little boy.

As Tommy's father tried to comfort his wife, Esme, her eyes filled with tears took out a whistle from her apron pocket and placing it to her lips began to play.
All at once the child stopped screaming, his head turning listening for the source of the music. Esme moved to sit cross legged on the floor facing him.

Unexpectedly, eyes alight with curiosity the child held out a hand towards her.
Taking the whistle a few inches from her lips Esme began to blow towards the mouth piece then drawing his eyes towards her fingers as they covered and uncovered the little holes in the pipe.
When she held out the pipe to Tommy he took the instrument into his hands and began to examine it.
Then he putting it to his lips filled the air with a haunting melody hinting secrets of magical places.

On the wings of the strain Louisa felt part of herself transported beyond place and time, through grey clouds until at last, as if penetrating a final ceiling found herself merging into the peace of an unbelievably blue, cloudless sky.

As the music began to fade Louisa eyes closed, almost imperceptibly found herself floating back towards her body.

When she opened her eyes she looked towards Thomas's parents. Had they experienced what she had?

His father, almost certainly as his face had lost the strained look it had worn when they arrived.

His mother's, however, had a look of fear and loathing. Standing up abruptly, without a word, she walked out of the room and went into the garden.

Tommy returned to rocking himself back and forth on the carpet.

The family stayed for two weeks in the cottage, the children happily spending most of their time exploring the sea shore while Thomas, pulled himself upright on two little spindly legs and holding on to the furniture made his way around the room while he lived in his own little world. He seemed contented enough as long as he was well fed and no one attempted to touch or press their uninvited attention upon him.

Sally had begun to visit each day from early morning until late afternoon spending much of the time with Thomas which allowed the rest of the family to enjoy their holiday. Although both Sally and Thomas appeared to pay little attention to one another Louisa knew they communicated.

On the first morning after she arrived, Sally asked to inspect the children's bedrooms. Moments later, like a little angry flame she came flashing out of one, holding an iron horseshoe and a pair of sharp, open shears. "Would y'm look at this! In his cot! An' in the children's bed!" she cried, brandishing them towards their mother who shrank back with a guilty expression on her face. "Ward off ...", she began but Sally stopped her in her tracks.

"I knows zackly what youm thinkin' of! Iron wards off magic, open iron shears forms a cross. You'm do more damage with these in a child's bed than any faerie would ever do! No more, You hears me? No more!"

The children's mother shrunk back bowing her head in acquiescence before gladly escaping the incandescent little bundle of fury, to join her husband and children on the shore.

"Never even looked at this little lad. Not a smidgen o' love", Sally said to Louisa and Esme, after she had calmed down, "Poor little boy!"

"Will you ask them, Sally?" Esme looked at her with a hopeful expression.

"Has to me dear, jus' has to".

For the rest of the day Tomas although acknowledging no one, contentedly held on to an old metal horse that Sally had brought with her and was supporting him to walk along the garden path. He ate everything he was offered and after playing magically on the whistle settled for a nap.

When the family returned in the evening Thomas's father together with his brother and sister called kind 'hellos' to the little boy accepting that he would not answer but happy to see him at peace in his own little world. When Thomas began to play his brother beat out the pulse of the music with his fingers on an old drum while his sister hit a few tinkling notes on a tiny triangle.

However, the unworried look on his father's face as well as the contented atmosphere in the cottage soon disappeared the moment his mother walked into the room.

The day before the family were to return home Esme requested they all meet that afternoon to talk about Thomas and a possible plan for the future. Sally had let it be known that she wished to have the child come to live with her.

Later when the family, Sally, Esme and Louisa presented themselves in the front room there was a knock at the door, it opened to reveal an elderly gentleman whose seemed familiar to Louisa. He was accompanied by another two gentlemen and three women.

"This is Philippe Elmshome", Esme introduced him to the guests after he stepped inside , "He's a solicitor". She went on to introduce his companions.

Louisa had unconsciously slipped her hand through her blouse to touch the little gold ring that hung from its ribbon when she saw the solicitor.

"Thank you Louisa", he said quietly to her as he accepted the seat she offered him. Surprised, she looked quickly up into familiar brown eyes smiling into hers. She was only known as Daisy here. No one here knew her real name.

Taking a notebook and pen from his pocket, he joined everyone around the table and after introducing the reasons for their being there sat quietly taking notes throughout the proceedings.

Questions were put to the parents and siblings of Thomas then to Esme and Sally. Louisa was asked about her impression of how each family member responded to the little boy and she answered as truthfully as she could. When Sally was asked if, in her opinion, the little boy was indeed a changeling as his mother had insisted she replied that she did not know but no matter what name was used, she knew she could give Thomas the time, love and upbringing that a child with his condition needed. She had done this with other children whose lives turned out well. His parents and siblings would always be welcome to visit whenever they wished.

After tea was served and Thomas's family had time to consider her proposal they came to the decision that they would accept Sally's offer. The solicitor produced written evidence regarding not only Sally's suitability to take on such a child but her success with many children of similar capabilities. Documents signed and hands shaken in agreement the solicitor and his companions left.

He had a few words for Louisa before he left. "Soon be time to move on my dear, the past is catching up". He smiled, "Till we meet again", and was gone.

Esme, Sally and Louisa waved goodbye to Thomas's family as he sat contentedly blowing his whistle at Sally's feet. His father's face was ashen and tired while his mother's eyes looked brighter although her mouth still wore a dissatisfied droop. His brother and sister stood by their father, the girl stroking his arm comfortingly while the boy wiped away unshed tears. As Esme and Louisa wished Sally a goodnight Thomas climbed into a little cart that Sally had brought for him to sit in. Then they stood by the door listening to the tune he played until they disappeared in the distance.

That evening as they sat by the fire Louisa told Esme that the time had come when she would have to leave or be trapped by winter.

"I feel that too dear Daisy", she replied. "My time has also come to go alookin' for my man. I've waited long enough. When I leave Sally and Thomas will live in this cottage close to the shore. I will pull on my pelt and return to the sea. Although I may not return to the land I can watch over them and sing with them and my sisters in the moonlight".

"Dearest Esme I will never forget you", Louisa's eyes were damp with tears. "Thank you for all you have done for me. I shall leave for the mountains tomorrow". Louisa joined Esme and her sisters on the shore that night, a trace of sadness touching her as she watched them dance and she brushed her hair by the light of the moon.

CHAPTER 12

The following morning as Louisa began to gather her
things together, she heard an odd sound just outside the
bedroom door. Her heart jumped in fear. Had the thing
that had been chasing her caught up at last? She'd hardly
given it much thought these last weeks.

Then she recognised a loud "Meow! "making its way
through the wooden door. Recognising it, Louisa pulled
the door open to be greeted by Siddi, black and furry,
sitting there rumbling away like an old boiler.
"Oh, it's you Siddi" she laughed in relief getting on to
her knees to hug him. "Oh I am so pleased to see you. I
have missed you and I've much to tell you?"
Siddi had grown considerably since the last time Louisa
had seen him. Sitting on his haunches their eyes were
now level.
"It's time to leave, I must find my way home, I've been
away too long".
The black cat's large golden eyes gazed at her intently.
"Oh Siddi, I didn't know what to do or which way to go
until two night ago.

I dreamed of a man, a beautiful man with loving eyes. He was in armour like that worn by the knights of old. The sight of him filled me with such joy and sadness. He said I must head north and west over the mountains then through the forest and from there to the spinning cauldrons.

When Louis asked her sea shore friends about the spinning cauldrons they described them as the biggest whirlpools in the world. So terrifying and dangerous no selky would approach them. Many lives had been lost in attempts to pass them safely.

Once she reached them, she would have to find a ferryman brave enough and skilful enough, willing to take her past them.

"Oh, too dangerous, there must be another way, surely", her friends cried, "Don't go".

"I must", she replied. "I will do anything to find my way home".

To reach them, Louisa had been advised to take a route across the mountain no more than a day's march from the cottage then once past the mountain towards an enchanted forest and from there towards the sea.

The problem was finding the safest route across the mountain and avoiding the henchmen of the old king. Then choosing the correct path through the forest was important because there were so many different ones leading goodness knows where.

After breakfast when Louisa brought down the pack with her belongings, she and Esme wished each other a tearful farewell.

"Does youm know where youm aheadin' dear Daisy?" she asked.

"I'm going home, Esme and as I began my journey by water and I feel that's the way I shall end it"

Esme looked concerned.

"Oh, not back the way I came", she reassured her friend, "I'm taking the opposite direction over the mountain then through the woods towards another sea lying to the north and west between two small islands where spinning cauldrons are to be found.".

"Ah", said Esme, "I know where yourn headin'. It's a dangerous journey but yon cat sidth awaitin' by the gate'll keep you safe", she smiled in Siddi's direction. "But be careful when you reach the mountain crag. The old king sits there. He's mad, thinks he still rules and a looking for unsuspecting travellers to imprison in the old mines.

Here, take this", Esme pressed a little black pouch into Louisa's hand, it's sandman's dust. Keep it safe and use it well should the time arise.

"And some gold for the ferryman too, he'll need it to pay the spirit of pool", Esme pressed a few coins into Louisa's hand.

After you reaches the forest, choose your path carefully. When you gets through to the other side an' hear a rumblin' an' a roarin' you'll know you is about no more'n ten mile away".

Louisa, wiping her tears, thanked her once more then she and Siddi set out towards the mountain.

CHAPTER 13

"I'm going home, going home", she sang to herself as she walked through high grasses blowing in the gentle wind, waves of green lit by delicate wildflowers of every hue. Siddi bounced ahead checking out the route before springing back to walk by her side.

Travelling until the sun began to set, Louisa found some shelter amongst the rocky terrain as they got closer to the mountains.
After a meal Louisa lay back for a while to gaze at the night sky ablaze with incandescent lights.

"Look Siddi", she said pointing. It's the northern lights. I remember my Mum telling me about a tribe of fallen angels that split into three.
The first became fairies who are tied to the earth, the second the blue men of the sea and the third the heavenly dancers in the sky who create the northern lights".

As they sat watching the wonderful myriad of lilacs, pinks, greens and golds shooting across the sky she realised these were not merely random movements but a definite rhythm directed by a celestial conductor.

Caught up in the heavenly music a silvery path of stars began to form reaching from the vault of heaven to the trees close to where Louisa sat.

A glorious creature of vibrating light gracefully descended, her robes flowing behind her. Siddi began to 'purrr' gently as she made her way towards them holding out a hand to Louisa.

"I am Aurora. Come, join us", Louisa heard her say, although afterwards she wasn't sure if she had heard actual words but their meaning, conveyed within the melody, "come, join in the dance".

.

Placing her hand into Aurora's, she found herself ascending the stairway. As she they drifted upwards tiny shimmering stars began to descend upon Louisa transforming her garments into a diaphanous, translucent, gown. A crown of diamonds and pearls adorned her hair falling in soft waves to her shoulders. Giving a gasp of wonder as she entered a ballroom glowing in the vast starlit space of night, she gazed at beautiful beings in gowns of tall colours of the auroroborialis casting their glowing light across the darkness as they danced.

The dancers paused, curtseying as Louisa and her companion drifted towards a being sitting on a sapphire throne on a raised dais.

"This is the Midnight Queen", she whispered as Aurora led her towards the glorious being.

"This is she, your majesty. The lost girl who seeks her way home", she curtsied.

Smiling, the queen graciously invited Louisa to join her on an emerald seat close by.

Louisa bent her knee and thanking her and carefully adjusting her gown she sat.

As she did so she became aware of a weak discordant voice accompanying the music.

Her eyes were drawn to its owner sitting on an ornate chair on the other side of the queen. An unshaven, ancient man with a crown lopsidedly perched on his shaggy grey head, his watery, colourless eyes gazing unfocussed into the distance.

Aurora whispered, 'He is the king of the mountains. He is very, very old and his wits have almost gone. His castle once stood beside the Black Mountain Lake but not even ruins remain.

With the first snows of winter he listens for our music on the cold starry nights then journeys in his coach to visit and dine with her majesty".

You will pass his abode on your way home He lives in a cave close by the deep pool at the bottom of the crags, taken care of by loyal servants. Be careful. Anyone they find trespassing, is put on trial, found guilty and imprisoned in the mines".

"Mines?" Louisa asked.

"Yes, silver mines lying deep underground. The workers do not last for long in those terrible places, forced to work until they drop by cruel goblin masters who drive them mercilessly. Once a worker is too exhausted to go on he is thrown onto the winter mountain and turned into an ice statue that melts when spring arrives.

Unwary travellers who are captured are tried and found guilty by the goblin court then sentenced to imprisonment.

Patting her hand comfortingly when she saw the look on Louisa's anxious face she produced a little silver pouch and presented it to her, "This contains the Sand Man's dust. If by any chance you are caught, sprinkle a few grains. Any living thing coming close to the sand falls asleep for an hour which hopefully will give enough time to escape.

Louisa thanked Aurora, gratefully accepting the pouch and securing it within her gown.

"Come now", Aurora smiled, let us forget unhappy things. There is a reason you have been brought here. It is to fulfil the greatest wish of one who has done us a great service. One who wishes to be with you once more".

"Louisa". A gentle voice whispered her name.
Her heart leapt.
Through the starlit night a tall courtly figure was making his way towards her.

All at once the inexplicable ache of loss that she was carrying in her heart began to fade as he approached and she remembered.

"Philippe, is it you?" she gasped.

"Yes, my love", lifting her hand he raised it to his lips.

"I thought I had lost you" her eyes filled with tears.

"My dearest, we are forever", he said softly, his brown eyes smiling into hers. "Come, no time for tears, let us feel joy looking forward to the time we are yet to have rather than back to the time that has gone".

Lost in a dream they danced the night away until the stars began to fade and the dancers, one by one, started to leave and they were alone.

Reluctantly Philippe drew her towards the top of the shining stairs, "It's time for us to say goodbye my dearest".

"Too soon. Oh please, not yet. Let me stay with you".

Louisa desperately tried holding on to Philippe's hands, but without conscious volition she could feel herself and Philippe beginning to drift further and further apart.

As if from a great distance Louisa heard Philippe say, "Remember my dearest, our love is forever".

"I need you", she wept, "Don't leave me".

His words carried on the grey mists of dawn sighed, "I'll find you".

The following morning, she awakened to a bright watery sun, her heart filled with a happiness that she had not known for a long time. Wondering why she should feel like this she tried to remember what had happened the evening before but apart from watching the northern lights flashing across the night sky she remembered little. However, it was with a lighter heart she set out early towards the mountain.

Although the terrain was uneven and difficult in places causing her to stumble grazing both knees, she was grateful for the sun warming her back and all went well enough until midday when it was hidden behind a large, navy blue cloud.

The air became chillier too and Louisa was glad that she had warm clothes with her although she did regret the loss of her white coat.

As the day drew on a bitterly cold wind accompanied them as they climbed the grassland towards the larger rocks.

"We have to find some shelter soon Siddi", she said, "or we won't survive this cold in the open. Look, we're nearly at the top, there might be a cave amongst the boulders".

Siddi bounded ahead towards the craggy outcrops and in moments reappeared standing on top of one.

Reaching him she was relieved to see he had found a cave, not a large one but big enough to provide the shelter they needed. An added bonus was the fact that a traveller had used it before them and left dry paper and wood for a fire in the corner.

Louisa soon had a tidy blaze going and unpacked the bag with the food she had brought. Putting some of the milk in a pan she heated it then added some oatmeal to make a thick porridge. When it was ready, she shared it out between them, placing some soft fruit on top of hers for sweetness.

Siddi who usually preferred catching his own must have been tired because rather than turning his nose up as he usually did at Louisa's offerings, accepted it and settled beside the glowing embers.

Louisa lay down beside Siddi, his welcome bulk sheltering her from drafts. She fell asleep in no time.

The following morning when Louisa looked out of the cave mouth the snow had all but disappeared although it as still very cold. After eating what was left of the porridge and bread, she tidied up then doused the fire leaving it prepared for the next weary traveller.

Wrapping up warmly both she and Siddi began to climb a narrow, wooded ravine towards the rock face.

It didn't take long and by late morning she had found a route that didn't look too challenging.

When at last she reached an opening leading to the ridge below the first summit, she stood gazing at the breathtaking beauty surrounding her.

The air seemed to shimmer in the icy cold as she looked upon the ridges and peaks of the snow-clad mountains surrounding the valley far below. As the pale rays of the sinking sun touched them every crevice sparkled with an uncanny glittering light and she could just make out crystal statues, a myriad of bright shooting shards of light emanating from each. How beautiful, she thought. All at once much of this beauty dimmed in Louisa's eyes as she remembered its source. The prisoners of the mines. Lives with hopes and dreams for the future. Were they gone forever she wondered as she thought of the them melting in the spring sun to trickle away down the mountain side to the streams and rivers and sea?

Gathering herself she prepared for the downward journey. It should be easier than the ascent, Louisa thought to herself as she looked at the scree covered surface of the descending slope.

Stepping into it she felt the small stones beginning to move. Digging in her heels she was able to control her speed as she felt herself gliding down the mountainside, slowly at first before gathering speed towards a black lake at the bottom.

Without warning the sun disappeared leaving her enveloped in an utter darkness that threatened to swallow her. She began to panic but as terror clutched at her heart, all at once a cold pale moonlight began spilling across the crags and crannies.
Relief flooded over her as the thin watery glow allowed her enough light allowing her to plot the best direction to the base.

Just as she was picking up speed once more and congratulate herself on her smooth descent, a tremendous croaking rumbled and echoed around the valley washing up the mountainsides in great waves.
Twisting her feet sideways and curving her body she tried to slow her descent but found she had left it too late and plunged awkwardly, landing on her side on the valley floor.
The roaring grew louder.

Light-headed she weakly pulled herself to a sitting position looking around to find its origin.

Aware of some movement in the direction from which the sound came, she was horrified to see great muscular creatures each with two large curving tusks on either side of flattened snouts their black, evil, beady eyes glinting malevolently.

There were six of them, each dressed in a brown leather jerkin and helmet, brandishing a broadsword and sitting astride an enormous, saddled and bridled bullfrog. They came bounding out of the rushes bearing down on her at an alarming speed.

Upon reaching her, two of the creatures dismounted and grabbing hold of her, dragged her roughly to her feet.

Although she stood head and shoulders above each one she was no match for their weaponry or their strength and had no choice but to allow herself to be prodded and marched over the muddy, rutted surface towards a cave.

"It'll be the mines for you", one of her captors looked up into her face giving her an unpleasant grin, "if you're lucky that is", he growled as an afterthought, his fishy smelling breath leaving her with an unpleasant sensation. Another of his companions gave unpleasant laugh, "Arr, if you're lucky", giving both her and her bag a hefty push through the entrance of the cave before pulling a curtain of yellowed leaves across, leaving her in semi darkness.

As her eyes became accustomed to the gloom, she could make out a number of large, thick tree roots sticking from the ground. Making her way over to them she sat down wearily examining her grazed knees.

What on earth am I going to do? I was warned about the danger and should have been better prepared. And where's Siddi? she wondered resting her head in her hands.

Half an hour later the leafy curtain was drawn aside and the cave flooded by moonlight.

"Court in session", a pompous voice announced. "Bring forth the prisoner!"

Two scaly, chinless creatures dressed in black gowns each with a white bib on the chest and moving awkwardly on what looked like flippers, took their places one on each side of Louisa. Another of her captors took up a position behind her proceeded to prod her forward with the aid of a sharp pointed stick.

She was marched out to a level area close to the lake. then pushed into a low sided box facing a high desk behind which stood a large chair.

On one side of the desk was a long wooden partition seating twelve odd looking characters wearing an assortment of scaly jackets and brightly coloured caps. She could make out two angry looking lobsters, one very large cod, two irritable looking crabs, one walrus, a squid who was haven problems working out what to do with his legs, three giggling prawns, a fat haddock and a mermaid brushing her hair as she sat staring malevolently at her.

This lot look rather fishy, to me, Louisa decided. Then startled, she heard a loud voice proclaim, "Prisoner number two and one quarter of a percent appearing in the dock!"

The voice belonged to a large mottled green fish wearing a wig and a long black gown and bib.

It can't be, Louisa thought to herself. I don't believe it. It's a court room.

"What on earth am I doing in a court room?" she cried.

"Silence in court!" an angry voice shouted as a gavel was pounded upon the desk and the stout fishy looking gentleman poked her with a large stick.

"Will you stop that!" Louisa shouted furiously rounding on the owner of the stick who was apparently enjoying himself and preparing to do it again.

"The Court will rise!" the clerk roared.

Everyone arose as a door to the side opened and two ushers carrying an ancient looking individual on their shoulders, a crown perching precariously on his wig, deposited him on the chair behind the bench. Once seated he raised his head, straightened his crown, gazed blearily at the gathering then, elbow on the bench placed a hand under his chin, closed his eyes and began to snore.

I know who he is. It's the mountain king, Louisa thought to herself.

"Who speaks for the prosecution!" the clerk shouted.
The large fishy looking gentleman with the stick
bellowed, "I do! I, Jasper Pike", giving the jury a
sweeping bow. They in turn began to stamp their feet
and applaud in appreciation.

"And who speaks for the Defence?" the clerk bawled.
"Me", squeaked a small voice, "Ooops! Sorry! I mean, I
do".
"Speak up, can't you? Say your name". the clerk
demanded looking towards the jury in exasperation.

"Oh, oh, sorry, I am Timothy Pilchard", a little
tremulous voice answered apologetically.
Rolling his eyes in the direction of the jury, who returned
his gaze in sympathy, the clerk turned to Louisa.
"How do you plead? Guilty or not guilty?" he shouted.

"What on earth are you talking about?" she replied
indignantly, "I haven't been charged with anything".

One of the jurors leaped to his feet,

"Guilty!" he proclaimed accompanied by cries of 'Guilty! Guilty! Guilty!' from the rest of the jurors to cheers and applause.

"Oh, oh no, no…p please wait…" piped Timothy Pilchard his denials all but drowned out by the querulous throng.

Someone nudged the judge awake. Gazing bleerily at the counsel for the defence he announced in a weak voice, "You have been found guilty by your peers and I er…er… " he gave a wide yawn, "I sentence you to ninety-seven years plus two fifths in the mines and I hope you are sincerely sorry for the wrongs you have carried out and will strive to lead a good and honest life when you are released".

Hastily the clerk of the court scrambling onto the desk proceeded to shout into the judge's ear, "Not him, me lud'. Her", and he pointed to Louisa.

"Who?" asked his honour.

"Her! Her!"

The judge, yawning, opened one eye to stare at the clerk of the court who bad begun to bounce up and down on the desk in exasperation, "Take him down, he's far too noisy, all he does is shout. A chap can't get any sleep. And while we're at it, make that ninety-nine years"

Before the clerk could resist, the guards surrounded him, dragging him from the court room leaving Louisa speechless and looking at the king who sprawled across the bench, snuffling softly.

Bewildered she stood there not at all sure about what had happened. All at once she heard a 'Meow' and there stood Siddi. Why, I think he is actually smiling, she thought.

Stepping down, "Let's get out of here", she said softly, not wishing of wakening the king.

Placing her hand on his large black head they hurried back to the cave to collect her belongings.

Dawn had not yet broken as she prepared to continue her journey.

"What worries me Siddi", she said urgently, "is the guards taking me prisoner again. They are bound to discover the mistake sooner rather than later".

The cat burrowed his nose in her bag bringing out the pouch Esme had given her.

Oh, she thought, I had forgotten. Perhaps if we sprinkle this around the lake it will keep them all sleeping long enough to let us get away.

Moving silently Louisa followed the instructions then accompanied by the grunts and snores around them they searched amongst the lower lying rocks until they found the passage that would lead them closer to the swirling cauldrons.

CHAPTER 14

To her relief, they soon reached the grasslands and when the sun came out Louisa felt much more comfortable. Looking behind her for the first mile to make sure they were not being followed she began to relax.

By late afternoon however, the sun disappeared and the skies darkened. Louisa was feeling tired and hungry but determined to reach the shelter of the forest before she allowed herself to rest.

"Looks like rain, Siddi, but what's that over there?" she pointed towards a darker shade of green, "that could be the edge of the woods. If we can get there before it starts that will save us from getting soaked.

"Run".

Taking to their heels it didn't take them long to reach the shelter of the trees before the skies opened and the rain fell in lumps. Once there Louisa paused for breath as she looked at the rain before turning back to examin the dense woodland lying before her.

Five separate pathways radiated in straight lines from where she stood.

"Quite a choice here Siddi. Before we choose let's rest on that bit of trunk over there and have something to eat". Making her way over Louisa opened her pack to remove an egg and some milk. Siddi giving a soft growl began searching for a lunch more to his own liking.

When he returned and Louisa had eaten and was rested, the time came to make a decision. Slinging the pack over her shoulder both she and Siddi made their way to the point where the paths converged.

Which one shall we take?" she looked at the cat.

Siddi however, sat back patiently on his haunches obviously unwilling to make the decision for her.

"OK", she said, "you don't intend to help so I'll do it myself".

Beginning with the far left path and pointing her forefinger at each in turn she began, "Eeny, meeny, miny, mo…"

Stopping, she swept her finger back to point to the third path. "Miny!" that's the path we'll take. Come on Siddi, and don't complain if things go wrong".

Easing the strap of her pack on to her shoulder she stepped onto the middle path followed by Siddi.

The path made its way by the side of a stream that burbled along peacefully over smoothly rounded stones. Tendrils of pale, fragrant roses blushed and twined around branches and trunks of trees.
Where the pool widened Louisa spied silvery fish lounging in the depths.
"We won't be short of food for sure", she thought as she looked at the fat juicy purple brambles hanging in clusters amongst wild strawberries and bilberries.
There's food enough for us all, she thought as she watched the sweet chestnuts, pine nuts, beech nuts and acorns lying scattered beneath the trees on the forest floor nibbled by squirrels while insects of all kinds, blackbirds, robins, jays and starlings feasted on the fruit fall from the crab apple trees.
None showed any sign of fear as they passed by.
Louisa, sure that she had made the best choice wandered along gathering berries until what light there was began to fade. She decided to settle for the rest of the night

where the stream widened as she could see what looked like a be a few trout. There was no sense in wandering in the dark and risking a fall she decided.

Siddi who had been bounding to and fro lay down on the bank gazing into the pool.

"If I were to gather some dry sticks to build a fire I wonder if you could catch us a little fish for our tea, Siddi?"

To her amazement it was no sooner said than done. Siddi quickly stuck a paw into the water and claws extended scooped up two unsuspecting fat fish landing them on to the grass beside Louisa. Grabbing a piece of rock she hit them both over the head.

In no time at all she had made a little nest of kindling from dry grass, small twigs and a few strips of paper, carefully setting them alight with a small flint and steel. When the flames had taken hold she piled on heavier pieces and as she waited for the heat to build she cleaned and gutted the fish placing them on a butter greased tray she had taken from her sack.

The aroma from the cooking fish was delicious. Siddi sat purring loudly with pleasure.

After they shared and tidied everything away, Siddi explored the bushes a little further along the path. Louisa bathed in the shallows and drying herself lay on the blanket she had taken from her pack. The night was getting chilly but the embers from the fire gave some warmth. When Siddi returned, he lay down beside her like a large furry pillow.

As she lay quietly, she was aware of the night sounds of the forest, the splashes of the fish surfacing the pool then diving back again, the snuffling of the little animals coming to inspect her then scurrying for safety at the slightest movement.

In the darkness of the trees she heard a soft 'Hooooo' sound and looking in the direction from where it came saw a large white owl perching on the branch of a nearby tree. Observing one another until the moonlight shafted through the high branches dappling all below, her eyes grew tired and as they closed, she clasped the gold ring on its ribbon she fell asleep.

The next morning she awakened to the sound of birds twittering and chattering in the trees and bushes. Close by three rabbits sat watching her before scampering away in fright when she sat up and stretched.

Once she washed and dressed she returned to add some dry wood to the still glowing embers of the fire. To her surprise three little eggs lay close to it, "Have you been shopping, Siddi?" she smiled, breaking them on to the buttered tin tray together with a chunk of bread.

Siddi refusing her offer to share with him and having his own ideas of what constituted a good breakfast wandered off to find his.

After dousing the fire, scattering crumbs for the birds and burying debris Louisa repacked her bag. There was no sign of Siddi but she knew he wouldn't be too far away and would catch up with her.

She wandered along the path for another half mile when unexpectedly it branched into two.

Mmm, she considered, now, which one to take?

When she considered the path that forked to the left she thought it had a decidedly gloomy look about it so decided it was probably better to stay on the right hand one beside the stream.

For a while it seemed like she had made the better choice until the stream that had gurgled and splashed along beside it began to wander away disappearing amongst overgrown briars and bushes.

Louisa paused for a moment wondering. "Probably best to stay on this path. It's reasonably clear and it's been fine so far", she decided.

All went well for a short period of time until she found it was not as straight as it had been when she first started out. It went back on itself twisting and twisting so often Louisa began to have the distinct impression that she had travelled along certain stretch of it more than once.

"I'm sure I passed this bit before", she said aloud as she recognised a gnarled tree hanging over the path. She stood staring. It reminded her of a green haired, knobbly faced, bad tempered old man, his long-knotted arms and spiky fingers reaching down to the path.

"I have passed this before. I'd recognise that ugly face anywhere", and she stretched up an arm to grab a greenish apple from one of the branches and took a bite. "Yuk! That's disgusting", she spat out the piece she had bitten off wiping her mouth with the back of her hand before continuing her journey.

"Ouch!" she cried a few steps further on. She rubbed the back of her neck. "What on earth was that?"
She turned around quickly but there were only trees.
She took another few steps when she was walloped again, by a hard apple, this time between the shoulders.
"Stop it! That hurt!" she shrieked looking at a crab apple lying on the ground at her feet.

"Who's got an ugly face? Look in a mirror and you'll catch sight of your own ugly mug", an angry voice yelled at her.
Suddenly she was being bombarded with hard apples.
"You like apples? Try these", and half a dozen more came flying in her direction.

Louisa, diving for shelter behind a thick bush, peeked out trying to catch sight of her assailant. There was no one to be seen.

After a few moments and everything appeared to have settled down she decided to take a chance and stood up. Immediately a hail of acorns, chestnuts, grit, pieces of branch and three empty nests flew in her direction.

Diving once more behind the bush she sat there besieged, arms around her knees, head down as she tried to think of ways to escape.

Eventually she took a white handkerchief from her pocket and tying it to a long piece of branch began waving it above her head.

Gaining a little courage when no further ammunition came in her direction., she carefully rose to her feet. There was no one around.

"Hello!" she called, ready to dive for cover should anymore missiles arrive, "Where are you?"

"Where do you think I am? You're standing looking at me. A word of warning for those big floppy things you call ears, just say one more word about me fizzog and I'll pelt you with the eggs too, and there's nothing more a troll loves to eat than a fat ugly human female covered in egg and sizzling on a spit" he began making sizzling sounds.

In disbelief Louisa gazed in amazement as the large tree she had pulled the apple from began to wave its branches in an agitated fashion.

"I'm so sorry", she apologised, "I didn't realise you could hear me".

"Oh, so 'I didn't know you could hear me' ", the tree mimicked. "You prefer to talk behind someone's back. Nice to their face but naaarsty when you think they can't hear you".

"Oh no, no, I'm not like that. Honestly. please believe me. I'm tired and lost and I spoke out of turn. I don't think you are ugly at all, in fact you are rather handsome with your green hair and... and long arms... and you are very tall", running out of things to say she decided to quit while she was ahead and ended up saying the wrong thing.

She need not have worried because the tree, mollified, stretched itself and said in a posh voice, "Oh yes, I am rather handsome aren't I! One has to keep up appearances hasn't one, although it can be difficult at times. Yesterday for example it rained all day, my hair got soaked and I just can't do a thing with it, and those squirrels are no respecters of persons. You wouldn't believe where they stash their nuts".

As the tree continued with a monologue of complaints Louisa would have preferred not to have known about, she gathered up her pack and edged slowly away. The voice faded in the distance; its owner totally unaware she had gone.

Two hours later after one more bend and the path petered out, she stopped, hands on hips she thought, This path's just one big corkscrew. I'll never find my way out of these trees.

Loath to retrace her steps in case she came across the cantankerous tree again, she stood squinting through the others towering on either side in the forlorn hope of finding another path.

Just as she decided she was hopelessly lost an unexpected ray of sunlight slanted through the gloom resting on what looked like an overgrown track close to the trunk of an ancient oak on the far side.

Heaving a sigh of relief she turned in that direction, leaping over roots and fallen branches towards it. "Thank goodness", she said aloud, "almost there", giving one last bound. This time however, she did not land on firm ground. Shocked into silence as the earth gave way below her she found herself falling, falling at speed into the unknown.

By some trick of time her descent appeared eventually to slow down and she was able to make out twisted brown coloured hairy roots some slender, others thick and many resembling the faces of old men and women lining the walls issued a soft, pale brown glow. A rushing wind like music wafted past her which she found quite pleasant and when she became more confidant she found she could adjust her speed as well as manoeuvre herself into different positions.

She found drawing her knees towards her chin and wrapping her arms around them was the most stable and comfortable and quite pleasant, after gasping for breath during the first panicky, head-first dive.

How far had she come she wondered.

She had been descending for a considerable time and it could have been miles. She considered she could very well find herself in Australia if she kept falling.

As she considered this her speed began to increase considerably. Alarmed she began to scream then all at once, without warning, she found herself landing with an uncomfortable bump on a hard, earthy floor.

CHAPTER 15

Breath knocked from her once more, she lay there for a while afraid to move. Everything felt damp and chilly and there was a slight swampy smell. Where on earth was she, it certainly could not be Australia. Australia was hot and sunny.

After a few moments and nothing had happened, she decided it was safe enough to sit up and look around. Louisa began to move but a sudden pain drew her attention to what would surely turn out to be a large bruise on her hip. Easing herself on to her other side she put a hand out to hold on to one of the downy roots covering the walls around her and began to pull herself up.

"Would you be good enough to watch where you put your hands! You forward young woman", an imperious sounding voice said crossly. Where are your manners?".

Startled, Louisa let go of the root and fell once more onto the ground.

"Ouch!" she cried, "Who's that?"

"Don't you know it's considered impolite to grab someone's whereabouts before being introduced", the voice demanded.

"Where are you? I can't see you", Louisa answered, narrowing her eyes as she tried to spot who was speaking.

"I'm right beside you", the voice said impatiently.

Louisa still was unable to see anyone.

Perhaps if I begin at ground level and work my way up she thought. However, all she could see were rusty-brown coloured roots of different shapes and sizes clinging to the walls.

Then she remembered the magic picture book she had received as a Christmas present one year. None of the pictures had made sense until almost giving up, she gazed at the scribbles without focussing and without warning a picture began to take shape.

"Who knows", she thought, "that ploy might just work here".

Edging backwards a little she allowed her eyes to look into space. To her relief definite shapes began to emerge. "It working", she whispered while she looked, eyes almost closing as she observed without actually trying to see.

What she saw were two extremely thin, brown feet encased in ridiculously high heeled shoes, long, spindly legs and an equally thin body topped by a slim neck and an angular head. Everything was a ruddy brown apart from the face that stared down at her. It was chalky white with blush pink cheeks, a wide, red lip-stick caked mouth and blue shadowed brown eyes one of which was covered by a long veil of brown hair hanging in front of it.

"Oh, I am so sorry, I didn't realise you were a someone. I mean a…" she faltered not wishing to continue for fear of causing more offence.

"I am Esmarelda Coltsfoot. And you are?"
"I am Louisa".

"How di do. You may lean on me to pull yourself up now we have been introduced", she offered graciously. Louisa thanked her and gingerly, leaning against Esmarelda Coltsfoot, held onto what looked like an arm was relieved to find it took her weight which allowed her to stand upright.

"And exactly what are you doing here? Were you invited? You should always wait for an invitation before entering someone else's home don't you know?"

Apologising profusely Louisa told her she was trying to find her way home.
"Why are you looking underground. It appears to me that you are a ground dweller. Seems an odd way to go about things".
When Louisa told her she had fallen through the ground by accident. Esmarelda tutted, "You really should not be allowed out on your own. What a stupid thing it is to fall down a hole. You sound rather lacking in intelligence to me. At your age you should know what a hole looks like and not allow yourself to fall down one".

Louisa annoyed, assured her she was quite in command of her wits and did not have time to discuss her grasp on reality and wished the inquisitive root woman farewell.

Esmarelda gave a "hurrumph!" before dismissing her.

Lifting her pack which miraculously had landed beside her, then wincing with pain Louisa limped towards a number of shadowy hollows each apparently the abode of a snooty inhabitant issuing rules of etiquette as she passed.
A number of thick roots hung adorned the walls while others were suspended from on high. Hopefully she surmised, the moment I can reach one of them I can climb and find my way back to ground level.

As Louisa made her way along a soft, warm light began to issue from the walls through the roots.
Looking upwards all she could see was blackness, I must have travelled miles down, she thought to herself as each opening she tried ended after a mile or so and she was forced to return to her starting place to begin over.

Hungry and her hip aching she sat on a raised dry hummock to take out what bread remained in her pack.

Without warning the hummock moved, tossing her onto the ground.

A large head protruded from one end giving her a severe look.

"Where are your manners young woman? Don't they teach them anymore? Don't you know it is very rude to sit on someone before being introduced?"

The head belonged to a very large tortoise.

"Oh I am so sorry", Louisa apologised. "My name is Louisa".

"How do you do Louisa. I am Terence. Now we are introduced you may rest on my shell should you so wish. I am going to sleep now".

With that Terence withdrew his head into his shell and began to snore softly.

What a very polite place this is Louisa thought to herself as she rested.

She was thirsty but as had finished the milk long ago.

Hearing the soft trickle of water close by she made her way towards it. In no time she came across tiny rivulets running down a wall and gathering together at a stony ledge where they plip- plopped on some stones below. Louisa extracted the metal cup from her pack and proceeded to hold it under the drips .

"Has no one ever told you it is very bad mannered to help oneself to someone's shower water before introductions have been made?" a squelchy sounding voice that appeared to come from the wall demanded. Louisa looked at the large eyes and lips glaring at her from behind a large piece of rock.

She apologised once more and the staring eye seemed to soften.

"Very well, I can see you meant no insult. You may partake of a little water after I have used it, that's the best place, over there, I only used that for washing my face", the eye squinted sideways.

By this time Louisa was too tired and thirsty to be choosy so she held her mug against the rock.

It didn't take long to gather enough of the cool brackish liquid to quench her thirst.

She didn't know how long she had been under-ground but it felt like many hours and she was tired and dispirited.

"I'm trying to find my way back to the surface", she spoke aloud in the direction where the voice had first spoken.

The occupant of the shower did not answer.

Louisa found a dry spot so she decided to lie down and rest for a while before exploring further.

She slept longer than she had expected because she felt rested and much better.

Collecting some more water, she sat drinking as she planned her next move.

Allowing her eyes to wander freely she gradually became aware of a soft, green glow coming from one of the passageways she had not yet explored. Could that be daylight making its way through the leaves and grass above she wondered?

Finding a stout stick to support her she made her way towards the passage praying this might be what she was searching for.

Stumbling along over uneven surfaces and through curtains of threadlike pulsating roots, she came to a rock barrier. The light as it made contact with its surface appeared to be stronger as her eyes travelled up the glow towards the point from where it appeared to start.

At last, she thought feeling the wave of relief that was beginning to encompass her bring a renewal of strength. Running her hands across the rock face feeling for footholds, she was relieved to find the knotted roots covering it would be strong enough to hold her weight.

After slinging her pack over her shoulder, she levered herself upwards by placing a cautious foot in one niche while her hands tested the strength of those above. Once she was sure they wouldn't give way she held on tightly as she hoisted herself aloft. To her relief everything held her weight and in very little time her head was level with the opening. Warily she pushed her head through to have a look around.

CHAPTER 16

"How strange", she thought as soon as her eyes were level with an emerald-green, grassy lawn on which stood an enormous piece of paper with the drawing of a garden.

Making one more effort she launched herself upward and forward until her arms and shoulders were through the hole and feeling the warmth of the sun.

Digging her elbows and fingers into the soft soil she managed to extract herself entirely onto the grass then looking back at the opening, she saw it lay at the bottom of a large oak tree shrouded in thick ivy.

While she sat regaining her strength she looked around. Somehow the two-dimensional drawing had changed to three.

She had landed not so much in a garden than a park. It was quite a pretty one with a waterfall a number of yards away, its water gathering in a pool below then burbling gently over stones before circling back.

There was no one around. Just as well Louisa thought to herself when she looked at her blackened nails and mud splattered arms and clothes, she could hardly ask anyone for help looking the way she did.

Getting to her feet and leaning on her stick she hobbled unsteadily towards the cascading water.

Extracting the bar of rough soap from her pack, she walked fully clothed into the cold pool and began lathering it into her clothes. Once satisfied the mud was gone, she removed then and after wringing them out hung them on some near bye branches to dry in the sun. The water felt deliciously cool against her bruised hip easing the pain considerably. Rinsing the soap from her hair, face and body she sank down into the liquid heaven, floating languorously as the tension left her aching joints.

Eventually she emerged to sit on the grass beside the bushes waiting for her clothes to dry. It didn't take long and when they were barely damp she decided she had given them enough time and pulled them on. Lifting her pack once more she felt she was much more presentable. After walking for about half an hour she caught sight of a woman gathering flowers. Smoothing down her dress and running her fingers through her hair she made her way towards her.

"Good afternoon, I wonder if you could help me?" she asked.

The woman ignored her.

Louisa gave a little cough to attract her attention then repeated her question. The woman continued to ignore her.

"Ahem", she coughed, but still no response

"How rude!" Louisa said aloud, then at the top of her voice, "Excuse me!"

"No use shouting, She can't hear you', a voice said.

Louisa looked around to see two young girls looking at her.

"Oh dear", she said, "I didn't realise she was deaf".

"Oh she's not deaf she just can't hear you".

"Or see you either", the other little girl contributed.

Puzzled, Louisa looked at them.

"Adults can't see dream people when they have their enchantment switch removed", the second child added, pointing to a scar behind the woman's left ear. "Once that's gone there's no more magic".

"Ours will be removed next year", the first child advised her, "It's a pity because I love talking and playing with the little folk. I wish I could keep it forever".

"But we all have to grow up and be sensible so that we can get on with our lives", the other little girl said in a solemn voice.

Louisa was quiet for a moment, not knowing what to make out of this talk of enchantment switches.

"Then perhaps you can help me? First of all, can you tell me your names?" she asked. "My name is Louisa".

The children's faces lit up, "We can surely help, my name is Lavender and that's Poppy", the first child pointed to her friend.

"How do you do Louisa", they chorused.

"How can we help you Louisa? Poppy asked with a radiant smile.

"I am trying to find my way home but I fell down a large hole beside a tree and spent a long time underground trying to find my way back out. Oh, have you anything to eat? I am so hungry".

"Come with us", Lavender held her hand while Poppy grasped the other. "Eat first then we'll show you the way out of here".

After a short walk they stood in front of a large piece of white paper on which someone had drawn a two-story house. It sat amidst glowing green grass under a pitched, red tiled roof. Immediately in the centre stood a chimney from which a wisp of smoke issued into an impossibly blue sky.
Two square windows had been drawn directly below two identical ones were situated on each side of a green painted door. On each side of the house someone had drawn a tree with a thin brown trunk and a mass of curly green leaves on top.

Why, it's symmetrical, exactly like the house I loved to draw when I was little, Louisa thought to herself.
She was somewhat surprised though when Poppy walked along the path, put her hand on the smudge of a door-knob and turning it opened the door inviting her to enter. Oh, she gasped under her breath, it's three dimensional.

The girls led her into the kitchen where their mother stood cutting sandwiches. A youth washing his hands in the sink flicked some water over the girls who screamed with delight. Louisa smiled in his direction but he did not acknowledge her. Must have had his enchantment switch removed, she decided.

"Can we have a teddy-bears' picnic, please mummy", Poppy asked in a wheedling tone.

"Of course you can my darling", she replied.

"And can we set another place for our new friend?"

"Yes, and I'm sure Philip will be happy to help you to carry out the toys and cakes if you ask him nicely".

"Oh, please, please, Philip?" both girls beseeched.

Philip drew down his brows in a pretended frown.

"Set the picnic and get the toys out then", he said in a mock severe voice. "Be quick about it, I'm going out"

"Come on Louisa", whispered Poppy, "let's go into the garden".

Louisa followed them to the kitchen and Lavender opened the door. The drawing of a garden appeared before them with a straight line of trees reminding her of green candyfloss standing on top of thin brown sticks.

They look just like the trees I used to draw, she thought. "Be careful where you step", Lavender said, "it took me such a long time to get the flowers right and the butterflies won't like it if you rub them out".

"What a curious thing to say, Louisa thought as she looked at little green sticks holding yellow coloured blobs surrounded by dobs of different colour amongst the bright green grass.

Suspended amongst them blue and red winged butterflies hovered motionless in the still air while lazy caterpillars lay on branches.

"And be careful of the bees, they can get very angry if you destroy their nectar".

What appeared to be five very large, brown, yellow striped blobs hung immobile in a corner.

These must be the bees, they are pretty huge, she thought.

"Come on then", Poppy said impatiently.

The moment they stepped into the garden there was an unmistakable change. It seemed to come to life as the grass waved gently in a subtle breeze. Butterflies fluttered. amongst the brightly coloured flowers as caterpillars lazily crept across branches preparing to join a number of chrysalises already hanging there.

Louisa cast an anxious look towards large brown bees the corner as they buzzed and hummed beside yellow flowers in the corner.

Once they had settled beneath one of the trees, Philip carried out the food setting it before them.

"Oh do stay for a little while Philip. We'll introduce you to Louisa", Lavender offered, "she's our new friend and you will like her".

"Louisa?" For a moment his expression changed, as if the name meant something to him. Then just as quickly he dismissed it.

"Sorry, girls, too busy tonight. Got to go", and blowing each of them a kiss he left.

"Philip is still a nice big brother, but he's no fun since they removed his magic switch".

"Yes, that was a great big gigantic pity", Poppy agreed, shrugging her shoulders.

Louisa had not realised how hungry she was until she began to eat. The girls, delighted, plied her with food of all kinds watching her eat and drink until her appetite was satisfied.

They played for a while, being careful not to disturb any of the flowers but when Lavender produced a frisbee the game became a little boisterous as it whizzed through the air and they raced to recover it and trampling down the flowers.

Suddenly, Louisa was aware of an angry buzzing sound coming in their direction.

"The bees!" Poppy screamed, grabbing Louisa's hand. They raced across the grass towards the kitchen door leaving everything behind them.

Reaching the door, they banged it closed behind them as the bees threw themselves against it.

Once in the safety of the kitchen, to Louisa's relief the angry noises fell silent.

"When will it be safe to get the teddies? Those bees sound very angry", she said.

"We'll soon sort that", said Lavender taking a large piece of white drawing paper and a box of coloured crayons from the kitchen drawer, "we'll change it a bit

Spreading it on the table both girls began to draw a garden. It looked very like the one outside of the kitchen door but this time they painted smiley faces on the bees.

"You may draw some flowers too, if you like", Poppy told Louisa handing her some crayons.

Delighted, she settled down beside them losing herself in their dream garden.

"You can sleep in our room until it gets dark, then when everyone is asleep, we will show you way to get home", Poppy said.

"I wish you could stay forever, it would be nice to have a special friend", Lavender sighed.

"But when they remove our magic switches we won't be able to see Louisa anymore and she will be lonely", Poppy's eyes filled with tears.

"But she could wait until we have our own children then she would be happy again".

"Take too long, years and years and years. No, best we show her the way home".

Problem solved the girls smiled brightly at Louisa.

For the rest of the afternoon and evening she tried to sleep but tossed and turned for hours until eventually she did begin to drift off.

She wakened suddenly when she heard her name whispered. Disoriented she collected her things and together with the girls, tip-toed from the room and made her way down the stair into the sitting room.

"Here we are", whispered Lavender. "The way home!"

Louisa found herself standing in front of a very large fireplace that looked totally out of place in the small room.

"Walk inside and look up. You'll find a ladder that will take you to the roof".

Not at all convinced this was going to work, she paused.

"Quickly, before daylight comes", Poppy urged.

Louisa walked into the grate, looking back she said,

"Thank you for all your help girls. I will miss you".

As she began to climb she heard them call, "Please don't forget us, Louisa".

Reaching the roof took longer than she thought but at last she could see the stars twinkling in the sky above her. When she arrived at the top of the chimney which proved to be much wider than she thought it would be she pushed her arms, head and shoulders through and was startled to find the collar at the back of her jacket grasped and herself being dragged unceremoniously onto soft grass. Looking up, she gazed into two large amber eyes, felt a rough tongue licking her cheek and listened with relief to Siddi purring loudly.

CHAPTER 17

As they made their way along, Louisa, attempting to come to terms with the idea of having one's magic switch removed, wondered if it was painful.

She thought how sad it must be not to believe in magic any more. However, when she thought about it she supposed that happened naturally in her own world as children grew older. Nevertheless, she promised herself, she would never allow it to happen to her. Magic was all around and people just couldn't see it.

All at once a low rumbling sound that seemed to come from underneath her feet disturbed her thoughts. Siddi, hackles, up gave a warning growl. Then as quickly as it began the disturbance ended.

As they walked Louisa once again had the familiar feeling of someone watching. Looking carefully to each side she was prepared to run should the need arise. However, there was never anyone to be seen.

As the day drew on the tops of the trees began to sway, caught in the wind as the weather grew colder.

Louisa drawing her coat around was relieved when she caught sight of a grey shape through the trees.

"I think that might be a cottage", she said to Siddi.

"Perhaps someone there will be able to tell me if we are on the right track".

Making their way towards it Louisa was pleased to see grey smoke blowing from a tall chimney. Someone must be at home she thought to herself as she knocked on the door.

"Come in", a tremulous voice called. She knocked again. "Oh do come in", the voice shouted. Turning the handle she edged the door open. An old woman dressed in a white nightdress with a red tartan shawl around her shoulders was sitting by a blazing fire. " Come on in, close the door quick. Got to keep the cold out". Looking over her spectacles she frowned. "You're not my Ellen", she stated.

Louisa apologised explaining that she knocked the door hoping to find someone who could show her the way home.

"Oh my dear", the old woman said, taking pity on her, "You look frozen. My Ellen will be here soon and she'll put you right. But stay and have tea, and bring your dog in to sit by the fire too".

Siddi was inside in the blink of an eye.

As Louisa thanked her the door opened and a young woman carrying a large basket of groceries entered. Taken aback she stopped for a moment to stare at the large cat making itself at home in front of the fire while the old lady stroked its head. Then gathering herself, she looked at Louisa.

"Who are you?" she asked softly. "You are a stranger to these parts I would think".

"I am", answered Louisa, "We have been travelling through the forest for more than three days trying to find our way to the sea that lies to the north west, where the spinning cauldrons lie. The roses faded from Ellen's cheeks as she and her mother exchanged glances.

"Well, let's have some tea first and we will talk about this afterwards", she said busying herself with a large copper kettle.

Gratefully, Louisa settled down to enjoy hot buttered scones and a mug of strong tea while Siddi lapped the creamy milk from the large bowl Ellen had set beside him.

Her mother leaned forward when she heard the contented purring, "Why you're not a dog, you're a big cat", she exclaimed, tickling Siddi behind his ears. The cat gave her an unblinking stare then deciding he liked this, purred louder.

"Now", said Ellen after they had eaten, "you say you are looking for the sea to the west and the spinning cauldrons? Well I can tell you that you are on the right path but there is no need to go any further north, it's west to the sea you will head".

Louisa gave her a concerned look when suddenly a rumbling, roaring sound seemed to swirl around the cottage. It seemed to penetrate the walls and ground beneath her feet.

"Not to worry my dear, it won't last long, soon be over", the old woman patted her arm to comfort her.

The noise began to fade after ten minutes although the vibrations in the walls and ground continued before that too diminished an hour or so later.

"What on earth was that?" Louisa asked when she at last recovered her composure.

"Winter's coming, that's Cailleach Bheur the Queen of Winter stirring Coire Bhreacain. But you still have time to get on your way before she can sum up the snow , torrents and floods and keep you trapped in winter forever.

"Queen of winter? I've never heard of her", said Louisa. Surprised, Ellen continued, "Why, she is the giantess who built the Scottish mountains using a magic hammer. She is the mother of the Scottish gods.

It is said she has only one eye, brown teeth and purple skin.

She bathes and washed her tartan clothes in Coire Bhreacain until they are as white as the driven snow. She stirs them in the cauldron until it swirls and roars and any boat sailing close to it at that time will be sucked down into the depths never to be seen again".

The old woman smiled, "You still have a way to go but you can take a shortcut over the marsh.

Why don't you sleep here by the fire tonight and leave in the morning. If you step out smartly you should arrive at the marsh well before nightfall. It's safe enough if you stick to the path and don't follow that Wiil-o-the-Wisp on to the boggy ground. You'll know you are getting close when you hear a booming noise. You will come to a little town where you should be able to find one of the boatmen willing to take you through if the weather permits".

They sat resting by the fire listening to the wind outside while the few snowflakes it carried brushed against the window pane.

After Ellen had helped her mother into bed and they all wished one another a good night, Louisa and Siddi settled by the embers of the fire and soon fell asleep.

The snow that had begun to settle during the night had disappeared in the gentle warmth of a pale sun.

After they had eaten and Louisa thanked Ellen and her mother for their kindness both she and Siddi set out.

As they walked Louisa felt a surge of excitement in her stomach and shivered, "Not far now", she thought, "not far".

But mingling amongst that excitement there remained an odd sensation of loss.

Although a chilly wind had blown up Louisa felt warm as she strode out briskly towards the marshy land, arriving at its edges earlier then she had reckoned. It was just before lunchtime and she reckoned if they kept up their present pace they could be across it before darkness fell.

Her estimate was spot on. They both soon reached the path leading across the boggy land. As she considered the terrain stretching ahead she could understand how in the dark it would be so easy to wander off.

However, they soon made their way safely across and Louisa was more than a little relieved when they reached more solid ground and she could see some cottages higher up on the headland.

Grateful for a well-earned rest after the pace of the day, Louisa sat beside the harbour wall looking at a boat and wondering if the owner would take her to the mainland. She opened her pack to share out what little food she had left with Siddi.

"Stranger here then?" she looked around in surprise to see a tall man in yellow oilskins. As she looked into his eyes her heart gave a little jump as if she had met a friend she hadn't seen for a long time. Chiding herself for her imagination she smiled.

"Here lass", he said, "this'll be better for you than dry bread and an egg. You look like you've travelled a distance". The man took a large box from out of the bag lying beside him.

"My sister always makes too much, afraid I'll starve. I can never eat it all and the gulls usually end up with half of it".

Opening the box, he produced two bulky packs handing one to Louisa.

"Please, I don't want to deprive you of your meal", she said, more for the sake of politeness.

"Go on take it, I have another one in the box", he pushed it towards her.

Louisa's stomach rumbled as she gratefully accepted.

"This is very kind of you, and I am hungry", she admitted, opening the waxed paper to see two thick slices of brown bread. Wondering what they contained she separated them a little to see that both had been spread with brown crab meat between which nestled generous helpings of cold, delicious looking white crab from the legs and claws.

"Oh, thank you so much", she repeated taking a bite, closing her eyes as she savoured the delicate flavour. The man took out a similar one and began to eat.

Louisa began to tear a piece off for Siddi but as usual he turned his nose up and wandered off to find his own fare. They sat for a while eating in a companionable silence.

"My name's Phil", he said. "You come far? Been somewhere interesting?"

"How do you do Phil, my name is Louisa. Yes, I've travelled quite far and taken so many different paths but at the moment I can't quite remember where".

Try as she might, she could not for the life of her remember exactly where she had been as the memories disappeared into the mists of the past. What remained was a confusing impression of joy, sadness, fear and hope. "Now I'm trying to find my way home".

"Happens. Not to worry. You're not the only one who's turned up here looking for the right path", he said. "You've more than a few to take before you find the one that feels like home".

Louisa wasn't sure what to make of this.

Lapsing into a comfortable silence as she watched the water it occurred to Louisa that she had never seen the sea behave in such a way before. Although it was slack tide she was struck by how uneven the surface of the water was. Rather than lying calm and smooth, in some places it looked stressed, like water boiling vigorously in a large pot then swelling and spilling over into churning eddies while in others it reminded her of the times she had watched the water from heavy rain burbling over some shallow steps outside her house.

Then all at once the uneven movement settled into an oily looking calm as a swell took hold reminding Louisa of a menacing, silent giant, its chest taking in huge gulps of air as it rose two and three feet into the air. She found that much more frightening than turbulent waves.

"Is it your intention to make your way in the morning?" Phil asked.

"Well, I was hoping to find someone willing to take me tomorrow", she answered, "Do you know of anyone?"

"I can take you. It needs careful timing though. It's unpredictable, no two days or hours are the same. Slack water doesn't last that long, sometimes just a few minutes then the flow picks up pretty quickly. I'm used to it though. Be around the harbour from daybreak and we'll take it from there.

I don't suppose you've had time to arranged anywhere to spend the night?" he asked as an after-thought.

When she shook her head he said, "My sister Elly has that bed and breakfast on the hill", he pointed to a grey stone cottage. Not expensive, comfortable clean beds and a good breakfast".

"That sounds just what I'm looking for". Louisa felt weary, tiredness washing over her.

"Come on then, I'll introduce you, but give me a minute to get these out ", he stepped into the boat ducking down then appeared holding waterproof trousers and a jacket. It's going to be cold and wet in the morning so put these over something warm", he handed the clothing to her then they began making their way towards the cottage.

The little guest house was warm and welcoming. After Louisa had bathed and changed into fresh clothes, she joined Phil and his sister at the table. There were no other guests so Emmy who wasn't busy was glad to have Louisa's company.

The meal was delicious and afterwards they sat by the fire chatting and enjoying coffee.

"I've put a hot water bottle in your bed, you'll need it tonight, Louisa", said Emmy. "I've also set the alarm for an early start and your breakfast will be on the table waiting".

Louisa thanked her and after half an hour made her way upstairs to bed. After a warm bath she fell into an uneasy sleep almost immediately, dreaming of a tall, blue-faced hag dragging her into the depths of a whirlpool.

The next morning wakening before dawn, she dressed in her warm jumper and trousers and went downstairs for a warm breakfast. Afterwards she went back upstairs to collect her belongings and pull on the waterproof clothing provided by Phil.

She said goodbye to Emmy, who after wishing her a safe journey, stood by the door watching her as she trudged down the hill towards the harbour as a grey line of dawn appeared in the east.

When she reached the harbour, Phil and another younger man he introduced as Joe, were already there. Joe handed her a life jacket and after helping her to secure it held out a hand to assist her onboard.

All at once she felt sick as the memory of the kelpies on her outward journey crowded her mind.

Masking her apprehension, she smiled and thanking him sitting quickly as she tried to control her shaking legs.

Listening to the engine start she watched a man on the jetty cast off then throw the mooring ropes to Joe who began to coil them safely on the deck as they left the anchorage behind.

As the boat slowly 'chug-chugged' along the sea was like a mill pond and the weather was milder than Louisa had thought it would be. Feeling a little more relaxed she looked with wonder at the soaring ridges of the magnificent mountains around them as shearwaters skimmed and soared in the pure air. Porpoises who every now and then broke the surface of the water travelled alongside looking knowingly into her eyes as if they had shared some secret knowledge.

As she grew confident enough to look into the deep she saw jellyfish and other dark, mysterious shapes flashing swiftly past under the boat. For a moment, her mind focussed on other monstrous creatures that might lie skulking in the black depths.

Without warning a stiff breeze blew up and the sky became moody as black thunder clouds scudded across it.

Louisa feeling her eyes drawn to the hills on the far side thought they were playing tricks on her as she watched a blue, swirling cloud of mist descend.

It began to form, taking the shape of a very tall woman, the woman in her dreams the night before. She gasped as it pointed a large thin finger in her direction and the once calm surface began to move.

Without thinking Louisa put her hand through her outer clothing to grasp the little gold ring lying against her breast.

The breeze increased to a high wind which began to blow against the flood tide which unexpectedly started to enter the area between two small islands at great speed.

The sea beginning to boil formed itself into many whirlpools from which issued huge spouts of water.

Louisa, struck dumb with terror gazed at one enormous whirlpool that appeared to be growing by the moment.

The boat caught up in the power of the maelstrom became unnavigable as the skipper fought to keep it from being sucked into the vortex.

All at once the boat was caught up and began swirling around at a tremendous speed. Louisa, violently sick and light headed cried out a prayer that this awful sensation would end.

Then all went silent and as she looked around saw the boat was surrounded on all sides by a great wall of water. Then she screamed as she felt the boat being sucked down, down into the abyss.

She was aware of was a rushing sound in her ears when suddenly, as she waited to die, the boat complete and its occupants were spat out in a huge waterspout.

CHAPTER 18

Eyes closed, fists clenched so tightly that the knuckles showed white, Louisa slowly became conscious of the roaring in her ears subsiding to be replaced by the background chatter of conversations.

Realising that the surface upon which she sat was no longer moving she opened her eyes. Disoriented she looked around.

What on earth is this? she thought to herself feeling her heart begin to race.

Where was the sea, the mountains, the boat, Phil and Joe? She should be with them, after all, hadn't they all been right there in the boat when it was sucked down into the whirlpool.

"I asked you if you wanted butter on your bun".

Her friend Julie sat opposite her wearing a questioning look.

Shocked, all she could do was mumble as she tried to come to terms with the fact that rather than finding herself lying injured in the cold morning air, it was evening and she was sitting at a table, in of all places, the Ashton café.

"Louisa! Do buck up. I asked you if you wanted butter on your bun", Julie began to look worried.

"Erm, yes please", she murmured absently. "How did I get here?"

"Walked of course. How do you think you got here? You don't half look a bit odd. Are you feeling all right?"

"So, we didn't go to Kilcregan?"

"Noooo, we were too late to catch the ferry", Julie spoke very slowly, "so we decided to stay here and go next week".

Julie began to spread butter on a large penny bun and cutting it into two slipped Louisa's share onto her plate.

A cold draft blew in through the café door as it opened to admit two figures. Julie waved them over, "You can share our table if you want", she said casually as they got closer.

The male voice that answered, "OK, wee sister, I suppose we can put up with you two for a while", caused Louisa to lift her head quickly in recognition.

She stared at the young man and his friend who pulled out two wooden chairs to sit beside them.

"This is Joe", he introduced his friend, "Joe, my sister Julie, and this is Louisa", his brown eyes smiling kindly into Louisa's.

Julie who had become all dewy as she said hello to Joe didn't see the look of recognition and wonder dawning on Louisa's face as Phil said, "Joe's joining my ship. We're leaving tomorrow for Singapore. He's staying the night. We thought we'd join you both for a coffee and I can walk Louisa home afterwards.

As they sat talking and laughing Louisa felt the shock and confusion that was enveloping her begin to ease a little as she remembered the advice someone had given her, 'don't worry, things have a way of working themselves out'.

Then, as had happened so often before when she found herself catapulted from one situation into one entirely different, she began to adjust and accommodate to the circumstances in which she found herself.

The rain had eased off when they set out for home. Phil tucking Louisa's arm into his said, "So you and Julie are off to university when you get the results of your Highers?"

"I'm not sure. I've been thinking I might stay in sixth form for another year and get the certificate of sixth year studies and apply to one of the English universities".

"Then by the time I am due some more leave you could be far away from here", Phil said thoughtfully.

When they reached her front door, Phil took a pen and a scrap of paper from his pocket to make a note of her house number.

"I'll write", he said, "if you feel like answering send it to the office and it'll reach me. The address will be in the letter". When Phil unexpectedly gave her a quick goodbye kiss on the cheek a frisson of pleasure surged through her. "It was nice to see you. Cheerio for now".

When she opened the door, she turned to watch the young man walking down the hill, the echo of a memory hung in the air, "Remember my love, I will always love you".

"Night Mum, night Dad", she stuck her head around the living room door blowing kisses to her parents who sat watching television.

"Night love", they both smiled as if sharing a joke.

"Careful when you turn back the bedclothes, you've a wee visitor who refuses to leave. I think we're stuck with him".

Bemused, Louisa opened her bedroom door. A little bump in the eiderdown began to move. Cautiously she approached and gently turned back the cover and out popped the head of a tiny, furry, black kitten with unusually large pointed ears and a white spot on its chest.

"Oh, you dear little thing", she whispered as it climbed onto her knee to make its way to her breast where it cuddled, purring against the small gold ring that hung from a ribbon around her neck.

I'd like to thank my daughter Caroline for the hours she spent editing my proof copy. I don't know how I would have managed without her.

I'd also like to say thank you to my friend Amanda for her encouragement as she listened to my ideas with such patience.

Printed in Great Britain
by Amazon